ConeBoy

by

Clive Parker-Sharp

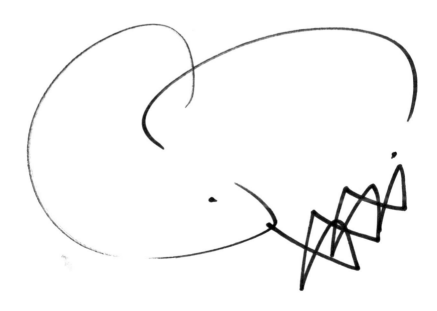

CHAPTER ONE - ST. PETER'S

Light has a scrappy chance of permeating the grimy glass. If it does

manage to leap the stained dirty window, it's rendered immobile at

first encounter with the tired thick velveteen material that passes for

curtains that had been hung there in a bygone era of positivity and

houseproudness. Half-baked roll-ups and joints clutched dozily

between the forefingers of innumerate visitors, passers-through,

partygoers, hangers-on (and those more interested in their own self-

appeasement, -amusement, -violation, -degradation, -elation, and, -

abasement), brush the curtains unwittingly. The material is grey and

seedy with burn stains, and pot-marked. They look like green

polyester soiled underpants strung across the huge Georgian frames

below off-cream pelmets that hide a curtain track which ceased to

function years prior, and positively arrests any curtain action or

possible useful application. Since they don't function they remain

permanently part-closed. Light that fights its way through to them is

filtered via the sieve, miraculously pronouncing itself 'arrived' on

the other side taking on a disco ball effect. If the curtain ripples by

what little fresh-air flow is allowed to enter the room, then soft muted patterns fall across the damask patchouli petrified flooring, walls and furnishings. No-one cares about the curtains, or what is on the other side of them as life is internalised, unnatural. Nature is imitated indoors, rather than connected with outside.

If they took the step of parting the curtains slightly, and wiping away the layer of tobacco and muck, a vista of overgrown silver birch would come into view, lining a once grand Notting Hill street. Along St. Peter's Grove roots protrude up through the pavement brickwork (it would make a great mountain-bike course, had they been invented). As it is, the aberrated blockwork is a solid deterrent to prams and pedestrians alike. It doesn't matter, as so few cars traverse the lane, residents spend most of their time lolling up and down the central tarmac, or what's left of it, as that's almost as equally un-kempt, and also a depository for local strays who howl and foul at their discretion. Weather is the determinate for exterior nightly pastimes, which vary from a few squatters and vagabonds hanging-about, smoking weed, twiddling their dreadlocks, engaged in meaningful anarchist and socialist bantering, to full-on reggae dub sound-systems erected at the drop of a hat, leads fed down from round two pin plugs on upper floors, energised from tampered-with basement Bakelite electric-meters placed in reverse mode by thick straps of red copper cable.

A multi-cultural melting pot, St. Peter's resembles every street radiating like spinnerets from Ladbroke Grove. The racially excluded alongside the financially challenged, butting up against middle-class ne'er-do-wants. Working families, immigrants, neighbours to doley Trotskyites, proto-punks, drug-addicts, aspiring musicians, new-agers, and hippies who'd turned a blind-eye to their own demise at Altamont. The disorganised, organised, disoriented, hated; a vast communal experiment barely bothered by the authorities. No mention of social-class, social-housing, integration, racism. A beautiful vibrant scene on a sunny seventies heat-wave day, freedom, movement, ebb, flow, no tension, no rules, anything goes. Greyness and British dampness underline its jaundiced degraded state, in the societal ladder. A slum, exemplifying pain, segregation, lost opportunities, sorrow, a dumping ground. An invisible force field surrounds. It's a place that's creedless, classless, The Leveller, an apothecary of incubating ideas and hopes, some that would burst out the hidden barrier, but most blown to the wind. Mostly it's a smell, of curry, dope, drains, peas and greens and broken dreams. A place to sleep, revive, survive, die, lay down and weep, a place not to be bothered and not to bother.

Surveying the second floor window, it resembles the others, easy to miss, even more so, that no-one was ever looking out of it. The paintwork, if you could call it that, not white advertised by a pristine fluffed-up dog on TV, but that of the hairy pelt on the back of an albino city rat. It has flaked, putty cracked, disgorged, and wood rotting. The landlord doesn't give a hoot, never stepped in the area, and property degradation is mutually beneficial to tenant and owner alike. The upkeep comes to zero, rent flows, and residents are left to their own suspect devices. Men in Golders Green have hoovered up swathes of freeholds here, sludgers collect rents, navigating the idiosyncratic habits of tenants. Little is normal here. Dues are allowed to linger, there's no extortion, promises 'roll-over' week after week, until one day there's a pile of belongings in the road and new lock on the door. Nowt said. There's a balance, landlord and tenant have an un-spoken agreement, pushing each other to the limit, knowing their boundary. As long as money comes in and arrears aren't abused. It's fair-play. The landlord leaves them alone, and they don't demand. Houses un-safe, uninhabitable, condemned, unusable, yet the demand to live in them unstoppable.

It's a location the milkman avoids. The only deliveries are small packets, paper bags, and items stuffed inside pockets by men in faded loon pants slung low, hardly covering their pubic hair, held up by a thick leather belt, chrome buckle, and bit of tummy showing below a cap sleeved Che Guevara t-shirt. In winter add in a Starsky and Hutch moth eaten alpaca knitted jacket in off white and brown that never quite ties up properly. Beefy necklaces de rigueur, religious symbols, Nazi iron cross, Star of David, pagan symbols, dolphins, stones, agate, hung from cord, shoelace, leather strap, or gold chain. No-one's fat, a diet of uppers, acid, amphetamines, LSD, mushrooms, heroin, dope, not enough time to eat. When food happens it's mostly vegan, vegetarian, 'alternative', something with beans, lentils, chickpeas, steaming slowly all-day, neither lunch nor dinner, or tea, embalmed in chilli, herbs, spices, that which can be consumed in a bowl. That happens between rolling the joint, lighting the joint, passing the joint, discussing the weed, lighting the bong, passing the bong, strapping the arm, inserting the needle, passing out. Everyone is on 'Mother's Little Helper', even the Windrushers who skulk off in the dark and return in the dark, who inhabit a space relinquished by the whites who've forgotten how to work. They wear the ill-fitting regalia of the grafting classes, conductor uniforms, porter's jackets, cleaner's overalls. Speed, diet pills, cannabis, double-shifts, night shifts, and Caribbean party weekends.

The window has little to endear it, except one of those hippy hanging coloured leaded light glass pentangles, bought in a cheap Portobello Road boutique, that which stocks crystals, wind-chimes, flapping cheesecloth shirts, low-level drug paraphernalia, coal Buddhas, dream-catchers, lanterns, candles, incense, runes, books on psilocybin, alternative religions, mysticism, paganism, and unorthodox thingamajigs. The decoration should be catching light and jiggling it here and there, making pretty patterns; a totem, a token nod at being 'different', 'weird', lives lived laterally, a world viewed through drippy eyes.

Roll your gaze from the window and grand ribbed-pillars descend from a substantial flat-roof portico, with fanned imitation Greek molding. Patches of plaster's crumbled and decayed, revealing the limestone beneath. The top of the covering, splattered with plant pots, is overgrown with weeds, dead shrubs, buddleias, and discarded bottles. The marble steps and entrance has long since lost its patina and cries out for renewal and refurbishment by young London upwardlymobiles, but that's years hence, and many years of decay and neglect lay ahead before Notting Hill would become a destination for City commuters and hip media-types.

The porch, surprisingly clear of debris, considering the inhabitants, has only a broken bike rusting against the left hand plinth. A large door welcomes and disgorges the army of liggers who traverse the stairs at all times. Perhaps that's the reason the porch is incumbent free. Boots, shoes, furniture, broken chairs, mattresses, and all types of discarded household goods adorn the other entrances in the road. No. 10 'trip free'. Black gloss paint is faded to grey and it isn't open or closed, just ajar. Security not a priority, pieces worth stealing have gone.

"I'm making breakfast, you collect the rents," Elsbeth says quietly, she of the worn in Marianne Faithfull looks, elbow-length blonde hair, long purple satin Biba maxi-dress, its billowing doesn't disguise her trim figure, legs athleticised by numerous public-school netball championships. Her blue eyes, crystalline, piercing, despite years of chemically-induced dilation. As she swings around toward him lying part naked on the bed, he catches a glimpse of her pure white cleavage, still ravishing, and totally desirable. The dark florid outfit is completely inappropriate for the hour, and she's slept in it. She cares not, such is her magnetism and eclecticism, and she may wear it all day and another night, vamping it up with beads or a wide velvet belt with huge circular silver buckle.

"Come and fuck me first," a muscular Italian drawl thickly draining from his wide lips.

"Django, if you want to eat this week, you need to do some work baby," turning back to the glorified camp-stove and blackened Butler sink that passes for a kitchen. Django pulls across the tartan baumewool rug that covers his lower half and reveals his erection.

"Work, work, work, always work, you'll kill me with work."

Elsbeth can see him from the corner of her eye, lowers the two cups of instant black coffee next to the dry toast, on the little drainer, and pulls herself back to bed in a way that speaks seductive and resisting in one movement. Morning is the window for sex, as there's a daily ramping of drug use, a curriculum progressing exponentially through the afternoon and into the night. They entwine, her legs encompassing him, the dress like sea lapping up against his brown sandy skin. They feel as they always do, in love. Django holds her strong cheekbones in his grip, she likes being manhandled, her breath shortened by some throat restriction, she arches back her head as he presses his other palm into her neck, her hair a thick mist swirling around the cushions. Perhaps it's her strict convent education, or inhibited middle-class parents that Django taps into. He knows her spots and she comes, which makes him ejaculate. He immediately reaches for a cigarette, the stretching only accentuating his taut body, not one drop of fat on his hips. At thirty-six Django is developing a small tummy, but his complexion pretty much disguises it.

"I want you to do more art," says Elsbeth resoundingly, which takes Django off-guard, stopping mid-light-up, the match not yet struck against the box. He thinks, looking across at the painting she's concentrating on, then lights-up, in a movement so gracefully cool, it could be bottled and sold.

"I'm an artist," he snides in his low rumble.

"Yes, but to make more work, another exhibition…. I loved that…." she rambles over him, interrupting, so gently he's forced into resignation. Elsbeth turns to him and leans on her elbow, gliding the other hand over her dress, like she's ironing it. He remains, surveying the picture, a Pollock'esque mass of previously bright dots and splashes, dulled by its locus. She continues, "You're talented." He puffs, hands behind his head, admiring his own work. "…And it's been…. Seven, eight… years?" He then speaks with the cigarette dangling between his lips, the ash hanging annoyingly precarious, his speech remains un-altered by the impediment, "They all know me." Elsbeth has a degree of lucidity, perhaps from the sex, "Yes, baby, I'll get a canvas, I know someone… some oils… I loved it when you were…." He manages to dampen her drive and aspiration for him, as usual,

"We all know someone, I'll get canvasses, just a call, I just need to make a call… they're all waiting, I can do anything….. LP covers… petty, meaningless crap. Just a call." She jumps on it, but more softly, and caressing his hand as if it were a delicate alabaster flower that mustn't be dropped, "Baby, let's go to the phone-box, I've some change." He looks straight in her eyes, striking her down, "You've money?!" He immediately rises, nude, her arms fall, leaden. He starts methodically and crashingly, searching her usual hidey-holes, one of the coffee's goes flying soaking the cold toast. She turns over, burying her head in the cushion, blocking out a scene she can't witness again. What few possessions they have are gone through, or thrown, Django working his way about the room. "I won't tell you," she half-cries into the fabric. Single room masquerading as 'open plan', and trappings one could count on one hand, bottles his search to about five minutes, but Elsbeth knows what's coming. He returns to the mattress on the floor and takes her arm, pulling her to face him. She's lifeless, drained of fight. He doesn't need to say what has fallen from his lips so many times before. She'd reveal her cash stash, like a clock that ticks. He pulls her toward him tightening his grip on her arm, but she has a speck of glimmer in her eye that's unfamiliar. Before he speaks she blurts, facing him straight on, head up, "I'm pregnant." He holds for a second as it goes in, then drops her, he immobile, she sitting bolt up clutching her head between her

That afternoon Django collects rents from neighbouring tenants, on behalf of the owner of No.10 (and most of the other abodes), with a kind of diligence he's at no time applied. This is his only job, and pays Elsbeth's and his accommodation. They've got the whole of No.10, but the other floors are uninhabitable, bar the people they let 'crash-out' now and then. The bathroom-toilet has permanent infestation; the first day's user would find large hard-backed beetles crawling out from behind the bath fascia. The only useful space, the basement, is soundproofed with egg-boxes and removals blankets. Django lets bands practice there for drugs and sometimes money. The Barracudas and Raincoats use it. It's damp, stinks, and it's deafeningly loud in there, the bass percolating up, as if that's the only instrument being played. Bands with no money frequent, and only as a last resort.

Whatever changes Django and Elsbeth implement, they go unsaid, as they never speak of the morning, and hardly of pregnancy. The drug use doesn't stop, they can't, they're too far gone. That would take an Alien invasion. Nevertheless, the substrata's altered. Parties are less frequent, the bedsit tidied somewhat, druggy toadies who aren't accustomed to a closed door policy don't bother returning for a second or third attempt, they just relocate their stoner's-pit. That's the good thing about junkies, they're adaptable. Drugs remain constant, everything else is dispensable. Any money coming in from Django's small time dealings goes in a tin, and Elsbeth takes the dozen or so paintings remaining from Django's stellar rise, back in the day, and sells them to dealers she's kept in touch with. Strangely, the punkettes return, knocking loud, persevere, becoming like surrogate fledgling sisters to Elsbeth, fussing around her, and attempting to get her off heroin, or reduce the dose. Elsbeth visits the doctor to get on methadone, he turning on her with a patronising lecture. Bought methadone is worse than the heroin, stolen from the back of pharmacies and hospital metal cabinets, then mixed with Vim, aspirin, and whatever else it can be cut with.

Few friends remain, most having been Elsbeth and Django's flunkies. Dozens of people reduce to six, including Johnno and Tasleen, Caribbeans living across the road, who Django had struck up a relationship with whilst collecting. Johnno is a mad Trojan enthusiast, spending any spare cash on dub plates and imports, to satisfy his reggae tooth. Django will linger for whole afternoons, smoking ganja weed from Johnno's pipe, experiencing his devotion to the genre, the dreads that are usually held up inside a green work cap un-caged. Each platter is savoured on the home-made set-up, housed in his upstairs living-room. Two record decks feed an ancient mini-mixer, then glass valves, juiced by four chunksome black-box transformers, tubes glowing bright when the bass lets-loose. The speakers are three-quarter inch ply-wood, painted matt-back, housing heavy-duty eighteen inch woofers, and two piezo tweeters each. Johnno sticks on a record, going through the musicians, sessions, recording process, studio equipment, then nods his locks as three-four rat-a-tat echo-plate, slashes one and three emphasis guitar and snare drums over the rumbling bass. Tasleen takes to carrying bowls of rice and chicken over to No.10 for the expectant pair, even though she can scarcely afford to put food on the table.

A roadie called Gash who can also play a bit of guitar is a long-time pal of Django's, having met him at a Roundhouse gig, before the site went into an ultimate spiral of dilapidation, a Sunday night package bill, The Pirates, Steve Gibbons Band, Brinsley Schwarz and Kokomo - when Django had arrived in the UK, and was lost for somewhere to stay. Gash had put Django up in his Camden Town squat, which backs on to the throat of railway lines pumping into King's Cross day and night. Gash stays up, preferring night-time - finding work with pub rock, then punk groups, he is now guitar humper for the Damned. Gash survives on Dexedrine and Bombay Mix. He wears a Hogan's Heroes Nazi hat, which guarantees a headwear related tussle when travelling less liberal climes, with Gash refusing to remove it. In-fact Gash is insufferable. The only reason bands employ him is because he is able stay up for several days driving a mini-bus across Europe, and still load-in a whole group's back-line. He hides his drugs stash in his hat. Gash and Django get on, fiery Mancunian and hot Mediterranean dispositions create an unpredictable pairing. The hard man act hides a heart-of-gold, and as soon as Gash discovers Django and Elsbeth are expecting he becomes Uncle, Godfather, and Granddad rolled into one.

A stuttering trainee barrister, Alistair Davies, who is little but the air barely moves in front of his lips. She bends her ear in all the way to his mouth, an act of defiance to his shyness. Elsbeth has that ability to break through. She insists everyone has a radiance, a chakra, to which she is receptive. True or not, Elsbeth has a way with people, helped by her coy dimples, and English rose looks. He speaks, she listens, she takes home a shirt, doesn't pay, but they become weirdo pals.

Ali now turns up at St. Peter's at a drop of a hat, after work, with another monologue of an idea, or enterprise, or entrepreneurial merchandising concept so far removed from his father's ambition for him. He speaks a subdued ugly South African dialect. It is painful and difficult to catch more than one word in five. They make him tea, he talks, music plays, and the Djangos' usual afternoon-to-evening rituals pan out. Ali opts out before serious drug shenanigans ever get under way and long before Elsbeth and Django jack-up behind their Indian carved screen, as more connections come and go. Ali never experiences the unsafe extent of their lives, and they never offer it up, knowing their demarcation with him. There is something endearing about this little ball of panicky energy and spirit, and he's not turned away. And so there are eight. A family. Punkettes, the Caribbeans, Gash, Ali, Elsbeth and Django. Elsbeth is obsessed about it, determined that there is symbolism. Star shaped Octograms, Da Vinci style Octagons appear, pinned to the walls, filling up gaps where Django's art had hung. Elsbeth spends hours fashioning eight sided shapes with triangles, cubes, runic symbols, tarot card illustrations. Django just tuts, more of Elsbeth's prophesising psychobabble. No-one has the heart to tell her they are actually nine, with the bundle.

CHAPTER 2 - WHAT IS WRONG WITH MY LIFE THAT I MUST GET STONED EVERY NIGHT

I was getting stoned every night. Fantastic, but not the best start for an embryo. If anyone says they can't remember occurrences before a certain 'age' they're lying, not trying hard enough. I can remember being in my mother's womb. That's why I never had a problem sleeping. I'm able to conjure the warmth, security, serenity, narcolepsy induced on a sixpence. Then the euphoria oozing through the placenta wall. Vivid spatial mind-expanding trips not intended for a teenager, let alone an un-born. Parental maltreatment was inflicted on me before birth, more psychologically damaging than any amount of post-natal abuse. Apparently they tried to kick it, went cold-turkey together, Tasleen and Johnno taking it in turns as nurse, between Johnno's shifts, Elsbeth's lump already showing, Tasleen stroked it, swabbing them from a metal bowl and flannel she'd brought from home. They sweated it out, a whining writhing mass on the tiny mangy mattress. Dimwits didn't know that coming off so quick could kill me. Django stayed off heroin longer than Elsbeth, but within a couple of weeks they were both back on full dose, the tearful screams could be heard right up the street before they'd jack up at around midnight. That should've been enough to put any locals off starting hard substance abuse, hearing Elsbeth crying out for the welfare of her unborn child, beating herself with hatred, blaming the man she loves, who had lit the fire of addiction for her. There was adoration, loathing, desperation, but primarily dependence. Johnno and Gash went after the pushers. They roughed up a few and nearly killed a man, but The Grove was awash with junk, and the Djangos had been plotting these denizens for aeons.

CHAPTER 3 - GOODBYE TRULY

"Goodbye baby, look after yourself," Django says.

A railway station is foreign territory for the Djangos and it shows. Elsbeth's floppy dippy look is outmoded, and Django's smouldering arty junked up sheen has rubbed off, his leather strides and puffy shirt distinctly stupid set against the polished September 1979 Waterloo commuters.

"Okay, okay, okay," Elsbeth repeats herself, shaking a little. She is on the verge of tears and deep maternal instinct has led her here, to the Woking line. She can still quote the stations off-by-heart from school-trips, shopping sprees with her Mum, theatre and cinema outings, Museum visits, Buckingham Palace, sightseeing, a jaunt to her father's City office, lunch out, and it now had that gut-wrenching familiarity. A part of her Django scarcely knew, only laughed at or derided from afar; middle-class, parochial, provincial. Poppy extract is buried deep in her garish-tasselled suede carrier, hidden in the lining. Three days' worth or more, if she can reduce the dose gradually as they'd tried to before, unsuccessfully. She has pills, painkillers, and dope to ease the withdrawal effects. Train doors clang shut, the wood and metal thunk ringing out around the transport cathedral, whistles blow, and Ali waits patiently at the ticket end of the platform, reading Oz magazine, his suit emitting a crumpled coolness like a black and white Lee Brilleaux record cover. He half observes his buddies, one hundred yards up the gangway.

"You'll be alright baby, call me, call me."

There's no way to call Django, yet he keeps insisting. They're unable to close the door, and the guard swanks past, flicking it closed with well oiled thwack. He blows the whistle again, and Django and Elsbeth, wholly un-prepared for this moment stand wide eyed. It's like they are both being orphaned, not having been parted for a dozen years. Django crosses his arms, a confused nine year old refusing to believe what's happening. He walks in time with the train, it picks up speed, their eyes locked, the platform empty now, another carriage pulls in adjacent. The part-open window of the door has a dutch-gate effect, splitting Elsbeth's torso in half, accentuating her petite frame, and delicate features. She seems tiny to Django, insignificant, the abnormality of the situation having a curious effect on him, like he is floating, unearthly. She keeps on

"I'm going to get the pudding, let me have your plate please darling?" Eileen fusses, in her standard attire, a plain white cotton blouse, with a small bow at the neck, smart black culottes, white socks, and brown sensible loafers. She's skinny, like Elsbeth.

"Let me help Mummy."

Eileen added comfortingly, "You rest darling, I'm here to help." Elsbeth starts to cry, and Eileen turns nursey, retrieving a box of tissues, that are mounted in a tusk box, from the oak side-cabinet on a lace doily. She plonks it by Elsbeth, and places her arm round her, same as her welcome at the railway station. She can't hug, as she is no longer armed for motherhood, having cauterized the empathy vein eleven years previous, when they'd realised Elsbeth wasn't coming home again. Eileen leaves Elsbeth dabbing her tears. Her gaze follows her mother carrying plates, serving dishes and cutlery precariously out of the door, then across the wood panelled walls, and the Georgian dado rail that halts at the patio doors, where she can see her father snaking across the lawns to the beds, having put on another pair of boots instead of retrieving the ones outside the dining-room door. He's holding a mug of tea. Elsbeth rummages the depths of her bag, pulls out drugs and eats them with abandon, how she likes it. It's hard and sexy, like she harbours a small sliver of devil inside her angelic torso. She takes her glass of water, gets up, and floats through the room, running her hand across the well-executed landscapes and silver framed photographs of long forgotten aunts, uncles, and cousins. "None of me," she murmurs. Glancing out of the doors again the sun is ten degrees lower in the sky than the previous day, backlighting the line of oaks, that stand guarding the border, two or three hundred yards down the gardens. That used to be her favourite spot, where, as a little girl, her Dad had attached a rope over a strong branch, tied to a small wooden seat, and he'd push her for what seemed like hours on end. It's the place that houses the shed, tools, mower, compost heaps, logs. It's where William is headed, his retreat, his solace. Elsbeth's eyes widen and she's rooted, watching him become smaller, having taken the stone path that starts at the tail of the lawns, underneath a climbing rose bedecked pergola, that sits dead centre of flower beds. Each year they'd be crowded with swathes of brightly coloured dahlias, the garden's crown. The beds separate the formal garden from the produce end, where apple, pear, blackcurrant, and raspberries dominate, before the raised vegetable beds, and then woody bold patch black and cream check, thin belt accentuating her trimness, matching Polyvore blazer-jacket, with teal and ivory piping, two side pockets, cream court shoes, white tights, swept back nearly Twiggy hairdo, dyed jet-black. Eileen made the best of herself, a forty-nine year old who watched her food, a regular at the Guildford Private Tennis Members Club, and Lightwater golf ladies team. She ensured she made the right balance of alluring and motherly to maintain her position.

They congregated at the boot, the Henderson triptych. No kiss from Dad, he held steady his patriarchal role by arms-length love, that of the Action Man, the provider. No cuddles or hugs. He handed Elsbeth her case from the boot, turning and clicking it back closed, green and yellow colours of the school emblazoned in two stripes encircling the statutory leather luggage. Eileen gave her one and only a huge embrace, "Have a fantastic time, and don't forget you're there to work, it's a field study trip!"

"Alright Mummy." Elsbeth turned and gave her Dad a peck anyway, he smiled, and said nothing, his usual shtick. He worshipped his daughter, just didn't know how to show it, his own father having been a violent RAF squadron leader, whose world revolved around suffering for all. Eileen and Elsbeth knew, and handled it. William tucked the silver cross back into Elsbeth's blouse, where it had worked its way out, a permanent fixture around her neck, and patted her. Elsbeth ran over to the breathless gaggle of classmates forming by the Bedford minibus, at the base of the double stone staircases that swept up to the grandiose school-entrance doors, enduring glass and twisted brass.

The Henderson parents were distracted by other parents they knew, flying into paroxysms; the City, business, politics, cars, holidays, property, the ever dominating wheel of wealth. 'Darling', 'darling', 'darling', it's difficult to distinguish which of the ladies was most effusive. "Golf, next Tuesday afternoon," Eileen broke the clatter of greetings, Rebecca adroitly, "Yes, two o'clock, on the dot, it's the best time, the morning hoggers have cleared out for the professionals!" Graham Stanley shook William's hand warmly, nodding to the mini-bus,

"They're growing up a bit nifty, shows your age old man."

"Less of the old, you bugger!"

writing, holiday duty for the boarders, lunch-time cover and long summer sports-fixtures. An energised five foot two, darting finger-ends, she had a keen figure, unspoiled by trudging school custardised puddings, and with swimming and rambling as hobbies, she had a lot going for her. Petite features, even pretty, auburn hair clipped across her forehead to keep the habit from slipping. Stuart had vitality, the Priory being her escape from an unemployed Dundee shipyard alcoholic father, it had changed her life, and she had no intention of letting circumstance hold her back. She revered Teresa Bartar and Ruth Barat, looked up to them, they the older experienced sisters, this was the third trip she'd volunteered for, and first abroad.

Teresa Bartar had been a poverty stricken spinster at forty and had abysmal halitosis. Nobody ever plucked up enough courage to tell her due to her sharp features, harsh demeanour, and the possible unleashing of a harsher tongue. With no relationship prospects, she skitted through unsuccessful Governess positions, hardly justifying a reference from any. Jobless, more or less homeless, as an act of desperation she found a calling, that of God, entered the Priory, consequently extending her childcare merits to basic teacher qualification. Sister Teresa was completely unsuited, having no empathy with children, and liked them even less. What she lacked in that department she made up for in organisational skills, management, and efficiency, very slowly rising through the ranks, until she was at least Head of Geography, a job that gave her a pension and a modicum of significance in the cloisters. She'd found her niche.

Ruth Barat could have been her birth sister, both in their sixties, not far off retirement, though they weren't twins. Ruth had a kindly granny disposition that we long for in a nun. Greying hair, a bit messy (unlike Bartar's), her veil and coif fell about, she'd frequently be seen dashing across the school quadrant, late for classes, habit flying, too many books stacked under her arm, ready to trip and let the whole lot fly. She had huge national health spherical reading glasses, gold frames, large red nose, a few hairs wisped from her cheeks, and deep indented laugh lines. She spent summers, and often weekends volunteering at the local hospice, befriending the elderly, and the dying, who ironically were usually about her age. Ruth was one of life's carers, and would be a Dame of the Realm before she hit eighty.

Over-talking calmed, fourteen girls lined into the vehicle, parents assembled, waving, and so I was on my way to becoming a living entity. Instead of the Rover shooting forth, it was the bus, pupils and three nuns. Only the black habits were visible from the rear, squashed up next to the driver in the front bench, no seat belts. Trees adorned by browns and deep reds, reliable English Oak, and Chestnut in the dappled copses rose up, sidling from the lane, into the Surrey Hills, a mist deciding to hang itself above the canopy. Chalky ground turned to mud at styles, cows huddled by gates, most sitting sensing the morning was turning to afternoon predictable drizzle then weekend rain, spoiling, disappointing. In the mini-bus gentle whispering rose steadily, each time halted by a nun's well-drilled chastisement. The nuns knew what they wanted, the radio on, and Luxembourg finally buzzed through a lonely single speaker mounted under the dashboard, fading in and out. They disapproved, but the music and American lingo'd DJs provided bones of civility as the bus wound its way up the A31, A3, and A30 to London Airport.

I'll spare you the Airport detail, needless to say, one can imagine, as I'd be told, that London Airport was more like a glorified Biggin Hill in 1966, and ageing Bob could have parked up for the duration of the field trip on the pavement outside the terminal building with little reproachment, had he desired. As it was, he hauled the bags from the bolted-on metal steps at the rear of the minibus, passed them to the sisters, who doled them back out to their owners. The rarefied atmosphere international travel created evoked such glamour and glory, the girls were virtually melting with anticipation. The nuns herded them through passport control, and they were free to spend what money they'd been allowed by their parents in the duty free, but not on alcohol. They swanned around the tiny store as if it were a cross between the Hansel and Gretel candy house and Charlie's Chocolate Factory. Despite being fed constantly, food was the currency at any single sex boarding school. Elsbeth and her two best friends, Susanne, and Amanda, emerged with duty free bags packed full of strange impenetrable Swiss chocolate, and repulsive chocolate liqueurs which they munched ravenously, loving them. They discarded the fancy packaging back in the bags and dumped them in bins before they got back to the three Sisters, who were piously cross-referencing the itinerary together over a pot of tea in the one and only restaurant, in departures. The nuns knew the demeanour, wide sugar-infested eyes, veins pumping saccharin round young pre-pubescent bodies, but they modestly cut the pupils slack.

Amanda and Suzanne looked similar, drawn together because of their height, impassioned sporty types, competitive in running and hockey. Elsbeth had started to blossom, from fairly bland beginnings. Her features were shortly set to become irresistible. She was on the cusp, boys would perhaps turn, and she would be curious as to why. Amanda and Suzi were more lanky and gawky, though it didn't diminish the boy interest. All fourteen wondered about the other sex, and sex, impatience to embrace adulthood draped on their sleeves, plainness their enemy. Amanda, Suzanne and Elsbeth made a great trio, on and off the pitch, the whole group were pals, hardly distinguishable in standard school togs, that being the object, the equilibrium that uniforms create, it gave them equal temperament. The three sat, opposite the restaurant, at the end of the row of seats where the other girls had lined up, chatting in the open and unencumbered way that young adults can. They watched the floating businessmen, homebound relatives, and the kind of holidaymakers that didn't need two weeks off a year as a reason to fly to distant dominions. White stockings akimbo, at a glance they were joined, controlled by a giant puppeteer can-canning their legs into all imaginable poses. There was no risk of thrombosis mid-flight.

And off they went, an announcement, big paper tickets revealed at the Boeing 707 door to perfectly turned out BOAC stewardesses, everyone squirmed in their seats, except the nuns who fell asleep as soon as they'd had dinner, having woofed the free wine. The triplets were seated together, and spent most of the flight pointing out of the window and playing a game where they pulled their dresses up above their knees pretending to be Twiggy, which held them in hyperventilating raptures. This was after they'd fiddled with lights, air vents and various seat reclining combinations for as long as the other passengers could withstand, and an attendant politely intervened. Eventually, the calming hum of plane air-conditioning and previous night's insomnia had the desired effect.

Elsbeth couldn't sleep, she knew something was changing, a feeling, she watched the lights coming on across southern Europe below, skudding over the Alps, white snow tops and infrequent single diode crystal specks signifying isolated outposts in the mountains. Suzi, white faced, eyes closed, high cheek bones - her German family had benefited from armaments in the war - and Amanda, of Scottish landed stock, eternally red rosy-faced, fired up, blasting-sapphire eyes, covered by the free blackout mask. Suzi's fingers twitched like a small mongrel chasing a large cat in its dreams, thumping its back legs. Elsbeth put her hand tenderly on Suzi's to rest her, or Suzi would have had one of her 'sleep jerks', waking in a terrible panic. It epitomised Elsbeth, caught up in the moment, she'd be kind, gently empathetic. Easy to see how she could be over-awed, influenced, taken advantage of. Another place and time could have put her as Patricia Kerwinkel or a Waco woman. The plane came to rest in Florence, moving forward to my conception.

They did their best in the heat, even the nuns were challenged. Compromises were found with apparel, and schedule, two churches a day whittled to one. Streets were motionless, the locals knew better than to flog-a-dead horse in an Italian Indian-summer, combined with a scarcity of tourists. They had Duomo virtually to themselves. A sleepy afternoon was spent lying in the garden square at Santa Maria Novella, tracing the timeworn convent gothic façade in notebooks. Thin white short sleeved shirts tipped over fitted narrow khaki shorts, tights abandoned, and sensible open sandals, all from Harrods, each item embroidered with the school logo. Pale green straw sun-hats, were accompanied by sunglasses of their own choosing. They were quite a sight towing after the nuns, who'd relaxed their look too. An air the affluent British high tier can pull off, of paucity, and confidence - they could have marched across the Gobi. Bartar, Barat and Stuart wore bright white long-sleeved blouses, but still had sleeveless blue-grey tank over-dresses, alabaster-shade leggins and closed black sandals. They'd substituted habits for starchy cotton head-coverings that buttoned at the back - nurse-like. A navy matching partly-elasticated belt, fed through four badly placed (too high) belt loops on the tunics gave them a top-heavy profile. This nouveau-nun style was a novelty, and constant source of mirth amongst the burgeoning pre-teens. The belt placement highlighted previously unknown breast form, and lack of bras amongst the religious order. Walking created a bosom-ripple effect, magnified by the cummerbund. Only the younger, Stuart, who hadn't yet suffered the ravages of age in that department, was spared the bottled guffawing every time they ventured on public transport, or in the tiny bumpy grey Alpha-Romeo mini-bus supplied by the tour operator. In any case, the nuns were obviously in discomfort as a result of clothing and breasts, so most days were cut-short, the students allowed to go in and out of shops in the squashed streets, buy trinkets, and complete their work-book questionnaires supping coca-cola through straws, in any of the numerous sunbrella'd town square cafés, whilst the nuns got shade, drunk iced water, read, and pretended to plan more schedule. Not much bookwork was achieved, as they laughed, giggled, got tanned, and contemplated the hipster, dark, drainpipe-clad smoking mod-boys dangerously skimming around the cobbled streets on clapped out noisy Lambrettas, staccato rock 'n' roll blasting from crappy Russian transistor radios bungied to the handlebars. It was heaven.

Days ticked by, syllabus indulged, important artworks listed, diagrams connected medievalism to modernism, many truncated avenues splintered off, which took up double-sided pages in their textbooks.

There was a twenty-metre swimming-pool at the hotel, and due to its secluded park location, they had permission to bathe sometimes, before dinner, if no other guests were using it. Semi-circular levels mimicked local church entrances, finely decorated riven oyster Florentine tiling, descended in to the irresistible waters at the garden end of the veranda. As soon as water hit the limestone slabs, lining the surrounding pool-paths, it evaporated in the afternoon roast. Massive locally fired pots resembling great Roman wine and olive oil urns, contained cypress, orange and citrus, bonsai'ed neatly into balls and oval. The girls bundled around, tip-toed across the paths as if on hot-coals, screamed, let off steam, leapt, double-dived. Suzi, Amanda, and Elsbeth didn't stop laughing, caught each-others' limbs under water, and took it in turns to swim through parted legs. The Italian sun miraged across the clear cerulean water, a Hockney azur, and fourteen girls tasted independence, like a joyous endless languorous adventure.

Ten days slipped by, The Galleria dell' Accademia, Michelangelo, and Uffizi, so it went on. The penultimate, a treat, a trip out to Montaione, the gem, dripping with mystique, bound with vineyards, olive groves, sappy rolling hilled woods, a thirteenth Century virtual Jerusalem of interconnected churches and chapels. A pilgrimage for the holy trinity, which coincided with the truffle festival. Resident and touring traditional bands would play on the makeshift stage constructed in the historic centre, in the shadow of the ancient fortified walls.

The shortish twenty-five miles or so took on the proportions of a sweltering expedition to Timbuktu, allegedly. Seventeen females and driver packed in a tinny tin-pot legumi can, steamed in brine, all style and no comfort, cobbled streets and post-war pot-holes rattled up through the non-existent suspension. The metallic unyielding openings were all ajar, and air blew through when they finally reached the outskirts of Florence. The sun was up, they'd spent too long dallying at the breakfast table again, even the nuns a little reluctant to get going from the marble comfort, and espresso aroma'd hostelry portals. They'd ascended the Palazzo's graciously crescented travertine amphitheatre steps, filed into the transport this last time, and they each carried a small holdall, containing a change for the evening out - not regulation, but their choice. Unrequited exuberance was reflected in voluminous chattering, prodding and rigorous bag examinations, scrutinising the outfits.

The driver, Mr. Alfonso, was mid-forties, smallish, swarthy, deep pin-point eyes, stubble nose, and a wide interested smile, that assisted in keeping tourists calm, even when the Florentine streets and congestion got the better of them. An unofficial guide and minder, the ladies relied on his local savvy, deep laugh lines baked into his features from endless summers tending his Oleaceae. Stocky frame covered by a messy grey work-jacket, two top pockets usefully filled with notes, pens and paperwork for making jottings on trips. He kept a note of every parking cop name, and would bribe them, embellishing it with a hearty laugh, for a space near whatever tourist building he'd been assigned to. The coat made him perspire and was glued over a dark brown thick woollen shirt, then plain baggy trousers with massive turn-ups, a little worn-out at the bottom from too much sliding on to the leather driver's seat. Legs were too short, rucked up when he sat, ramming the vehicle into gears it didn't know existed, revealed shins, washed-out black socks, and plain brown shoes like cricket boots. He'd been a successful farmer, and lost everything in Mafioso wars, his objections to forced labour foisted on him found him sitting amongst an inferno made from his two hundred year old olive trees one night. And so his brother-in-law got him a job in the city, driving mini-buses for tourists. He quickly picked up a soupçon of German, English and French, and it got him through. Being able to handle a tractor was useful in these streets. He really got in his stride out in the country, his limbs a slew of animated action, right arm ripping the gear lever about to navigate the sharp turns, and hair-pin bends, then finally the Groma straightened avenues.

A few of the students were familiar with the sight of peasants toiling in the groves and plots that made up the innumerate blanched stone-wall separated allotments. They'd seen agricultural workers on family holidays, several had been to Italy before. It hadn't lost its appeal, the hunched labourers cut, fed, watered, dug, harvested, often so low to the soil that they were the land and the land was them, fused in the eternal relationship, man and earth. They were shaded from the mid-morning blaze with worn out hats, neckerchiefs, scarves, and deep brown grizzled faces hardly startled by passing vehicles. It was impossible to picture without a romantic tinge, a soulful tingle of admiration.

Alfonso proceeded, the females digested, air blew through, ponytails, pigtails, pixie, bobs, and locks fluffed in the breeze and the majesty of Montaione reared up in the distance. As acceleration had no effect on the soaring discomfort levels in the cooker, they stopped more times than really necessary. A pokey roadside lorry stop, which mainly slopped out five lire shots of wine (that resembled short sherry tumblers), to the olive-oil tank drivers, alongside plates of heavily salted anchovies and a thick wad of local bread for twenty lire. Two thousand litre mini-tankers, pulled by aging Fiat diesel units zipped along tracks collecting the liquid gold pressed from the fruit of bountiful olive-trees in these hillsides. They'd be transferred to the central co-op, an ancient factory at Sienna, filtered, graded, bottled and shipped out to bigger plants for distribution, operations carefully overseen and wrangled over by a network of organised crime families. The bus blew up dust as it careered into the small olive and fig tree encamped car-park, and Alfonso slugged off the ignition and radio which had been broadcasting the national diet of pappy love songs and generic divas - not quite as good as Dean Martin, who they aspired to. The radio was the only decent component in the Alpha-Romeo, and the girls loved the ludicrous high-pitched wailing and deep cellos that boomed out of the big speakers.

The group trooped through to the dirty toilet, a hole in the ground disguised with a primitive porcelain commode, accommodating foot-holes either side. The few drivers lunching didn't bat an eyelid from the brightly decorated pvc wipeable tablecloths, as if it was perfectly normal, nuns consistently offering a kind of acceptance to the bizarre sight. This was taken as an opportunity to have an early lunch, cold bottles of pop bought from the bemused counter girl, virtually the same age as the conventeers, but a universe apart. The girls patronisingly practised their Italian, but her dialect was impenetrable. Ridiculously large notes were handed over, thousands, amusingly, amounted to pence, such was the state of the economy. Nuns and pupils found cool spots on pockets of vivid wild-meadow grass, at the periphery of the car-park, where smallholdings started, under trees, leaning against the shaded limestone walls, and watched zingy green geckos dart between the cracks. They laid out the hotel packed lunches, ham and cheese sandwiches and fruit, spreading the foil and brown paper wrapping on the grass to put the food on. A black cat with one white splurge on its neck slunk over from the taverna, and they witnessed a dozen or so trucks, and one car, pull in and out, heaving up a mustardy fumey haze in their wake, far enough from the troupe to imagine they were in a scene from a Vittoria De Sica movie. Men hung-around, not punching the clock, smoked, chatted idly, each a unique work jacket that signified their haulage firm. Alfonso chain-smoked in the cab of the taxibus, door open, legs dangled out, neither in-nor-out, he surveyed the transport restaurant. He knew some of the drivers and waved laconically, his chauffer role a million miles from the one he'd inhabited before. He waited patiently on his horde, puffing slowly on Virginia Pelicans. Half a dozen went and bought more pop as an excuse to pump the jukebox they'd seen in the bar, skipping off, the thirty degree heat not registering, and the three friends played with the cat. Elsbeth grasped long stems of grass which she wiggled, and the cat ramped around after the fluffy end as if it were a field mouse darting though undergrowth. It wanted food, but that was gone, the girls seldom missed any advantage to eat their bodyweight, even though it was only a while since breakfast.

They lingered, a gritty authenticity that held them there, watching a slice of Italian arcadia they wouldn't witness again. Artworks and churches were immovable, but this scintilla was a one-off, primeval, ancient towers of Montaione on the horizon, the surrounding peaks of Appenine rising, awaiting their first winter smattering of white frosted snowfall, tick-tock of life in the ether.

The other five girls and nuns were animatedly chatting, the teacher-pupil barrier erased, women, bonded. 'Jukebox group' eventually wandered back, they'd picked small bunches of wild flowers, piercing turquoise Muscari Neglectum, and dainty mini-tulips. They'd be wilting within a couple of hours, and the nuns ignored it. The detritus was cleared and packed into the mini-bus. There were no rubbish bins, and the car-park already had enough litter. Alphoso closed the doors on the passengers, went to the driver's side, choked the engine into action, and they left. The atmosphere had changed from incessant youthful banter, an odd preternatural transformation. The bassy speaker still chundered out the continuous programme of vanilla middle-of-the-road, but there was reticence in the air, a tilt. Like the last day of school, or final parting of a divorcing couple, end colliding with start, the tide shifted for all of them.

The town was full-on busy, stalls displayed local white fungi, lush produce, touristy crafts, and a grand, rather rickety looking wooden stand in the main square, overlooked by the quaint church of San Regolo. A train of coloured bulbs was fringing the front of the stage, and there were two WEM columns, housing four large twelve inch speakers each, one either side of the stand, to amplify the singing into the echoing piazza. The town banner covered the stage-front, the coat of arms painted proudly in the centre. Cafés were open, buzzing, atmosphere jolly, seemingly livelier than Florence had been, the hills cooler than the blistering city. Local producers came from every corner of Tuscany to show, for fancy little trophies, certificates, rosettes, and colourful ribbons, handed out by the local Mayor and a few dignitaries, at seven in the evening, when the heat had dissipated. Then the concert would strike up, there'd be drink, dance, and the centuries old market town tradition could play out.

The party schlepped round the church, documenting the Madonna del Buonconsiglio, the Holy Mount and convent of San Vivaldo, with numerous important religious icons to ponder. Their hearts, and even that of the nuns, weren't quite in it, all looking forward to getting dressed up and enjoying the evening's entertainment. The girls persevered, pencils ardently scribbled interpretations, and records, to be transferred into major projects in large leaf folders when they returned to England. They knew they had to do the work, and keyed each-other on, whispered about outfits, what they'd look like, and whether Sister Stuart would let them dance. Elsbeth, Suzi and Amanda already had moves, ad-hoc practicing in front of religious imagery that required hushed contemplation wasn't appreciated. Bartar, Barat, and Stuart split up, their protocol of splintering in to three groups aided concentration, and the students were rapidly steered back to their modus operandi.

The nuns had made a special arrangement with the monastery, now a school, and part of an informal student exchange network. At five, they drove a short distance to the impressive stone building jutting on an escarpment at the edge of the town; a tarmaced single-lane road lead up to the front drive and tidy parking area, an elaborate equine inspired fountain in the middle. Buildings were a hotchpotch, but well-kept, a few modernised, others refurbished. Vineyards sloped for as far as one could see. The bursar, a suited, tall, fresh looking middle-aged man was already waiting in the rocky portico, and he showed them to the old wash houses, converted to changing rooms for sports-hall periods. Friendly and efficient and not what the nuns had been expecting, he mainly spoke fast parlance to Alphonso, with little English. He was anxious to escape, and left the large key with Alphonso to post back through the letterbox when they'd finished, precisely instructing on the peculiarities of the mature mechanism. The young-ladies took their bags, washed in the stainless steel sinks, not much hot water, as the boiler was now turned off for the evening, but they didn't notice, such was their rapture at getting dressed up and going out on the town. Instructions had been issued as to what was admissible casual wear, which had invoked gargantuan levels of debate and negotiation in homes across

Surrey; mainly girls haranguing their mothers. The no-man's-land

between acceptable and risqué pushed to the limit by the insistent

persistence of fourteen adolescents growing up in a fashion

whirlwind era. A wild vogue-ish parade was on the cards, like an

insane dress-down Friday, and a number had sneaked make-up.

Long wooden benches butted the wall, down the edge of the musty

changing-rooms, salt and soap soaked stonework still retaining its

odour from when the buildings had been the manual laundry for the

monks. Metal locker cabinets stood at one end, and hooks, where

two sad gym-slips had been left behind. There weren't any mirrors,

but the steel splashbacks of the sinks reflected with a bit of

persuasive elbow-grease with the gym-slips. They vamped, and

posed, creating fits of laughter, and could be heard across the

campus, but no-one being there, it didn't matter. It was the time of

their lives, every move and word vital; a seared fabulous celebration

of friendship and love.

The nuns stood with Alphoso by the bus in the limestone-

chipped lot, awaited their turn, admired the view, and relished the cooling afternoon. The travel agent had booked food at a local restaurant for 7 pm, there was no reason to rush, it was just five minutes into town. Mary Stuart braced herself, and went to unleash the cacophony of fad, texture, mishmash, textile and pigment into the world. She strolled across the park, chippings crunching under leather soles, skirterall brushing the inside of her thighs - approached the heavy wooden door, and tentatively depressed the large brass handle. Noise hit her as she arced her head round the door. In a clear Scottish brawl, "Collect your bags and everyone out please!" up-tailing the end of the sentence, so it couldn't be interrupted or misinterpreted. Stuart swung the door right back and the parade begun.

First the five 'nunny' girls, a fairly bookish lot, who preferred the company of the 'holy three', hanging on every paraphrase and religious insight. They had skirts, one slacks, varying degrees of plain and tartan, snazzy little crocheted and polka-dot tops, kitten heels, and white tights. Then the Jukebox six, a tad more daring and hipster, bright red and black mini-skirts, with a skewed big-print tartan, like the leaning tower of Pisa. They had fresh white blousy frilled shirts interrupted by wide, high waistbands, the skirts obviously raised too far, revealing knees and thighs, even go-go boots. A few had eyeliner, all with lipstick. Sporty three trouped behind, and there was the shock. Gangly, gawky and lanky had disappeared, replaced by shimmer, shammy, shake. Suzi wore a psychedelic dress, horizontal stripes of random thickness, browns faded into bright oranges and purples, and circled her long elegant structure. Her bob, usually a mess of ruffled vigour was clipped behind her ears, blonde streaks from the chlorine and sun burnt into her brunette locks. Suzanne's Germanic heritage had unmasked, as a young woman. Long brown legs with perfectly formed calves fell to thin ankles and backless sandals with a slight heel. Amanda used her hair as a crutch invariably, but she'd pulled it off her face with an Indian print Alice-band. It slimmed reddy cheeks, now browned, flame wild hair freed over her shoulders. A floaty gypsy dress bought from Samantha's boutique in Guildford, in one of the alleys that connected the two steep high-streets. Black boots went up to her knees with chunky heels, buttoned on the outside. Elsbeth had an all-in-one ivory jumpsuit on, swishing cool baggy legs that stopped short, revealing her ankles and flattish silvery sandals. The front was cross-hatch v, eyelets ran up from her belly button, two long laces criss-crossed her flesh, and tied in a bow above her sternum. The knot was yearning to be opened, she was sumptuous. The long glimpse of skin from her stomach complimented Elsbeth's lack of breasts. Long sleeves flared out and ruffles framed her delicate wrists. Elsbeth's hair was infrequently out of ponytails, and the tight weave formed a cadence of waves and shades when let-loose. It was a river sprung from a dam, gushing spray danced over her cheeks and shoulders, bright blonde, almost white from the sun. All the girls looked amazing, breeding, private education, good food, sport, and poise their calling card.

A catwalk across the court ensued, the girls clung on to each-other, giggled, unsteady in heels, not assisted by the gritty passage. Alphonso was astonished, his eyes stalked. He'd seen a few sights in his years ferrying sightseers, but this was quite a transformation after bland school scrubs. They bunched neatly by the mini-bus where the nuns made subtle suggestions, a few top buttons done up and skirts restored to their proper length. The make-up was ignored, the nuns had a side confab and concluded it would be too dark for anyone to notice anyway. The nuns went and washed, and came back exactly the same, but freshened up, then last in turn, Alphonso. He gave himself a full flannel rub, and appeared in reasonable looking denims and a clean white shirt. He could've been ten years younger, the girls giving applause, even causing the semi-serious nuns to smile. He bowed, whisked his cigarette pack from the dashboard, lit up, and the bus crunched out of the courtyard. Alphonso got about ten yards, pulled up the handbrake, retrieved the big key from his pocket, holding it up to the Sisters. He levered open the door, and jogged up the hill, deposited the key, as promised, jogged back, fag still burning in his lips, a little out-of-breath, and they departed for town.

The restaurant was a tavern, on the corner of one of the closed-in crowded streets that met the central piazza. Food was basic, local wine free with the meal, carafes full of the enticing red liquid dotted the joined-up tables. The girls were allowed a taste of wine, heavily diluted, Bartar and Barat poured, to be certain of quantity. They preferred the coca-cola, not yet warmed to the benefits of alcohol. The nuns couldn't resist, the jugs melted away, the relief at having completed their trip duties, and rewarded themselves on the last night. A meal was taken out to Alphonso, who preferred to shadow the bus. He had his own wine bottle in the driver's door pocket that he swigged from. The usual wipe-off brightly decorated table-cloths were covered with large baskets of artisan bread, and two courses of a heavily reduced sauce varnished local beef, and salad, which was wolfed down, then dessert, irresistible glutinous deep-fried biscuits, fluffed in icing-sugar. The gang were particularly careful not to splash their clothes. They could see the awards ceremony through the window, bulbs sparkled above the piazza cafés as dark descended, and the first band cranked into action. It was ethnic folky music in three-four time, a flute, lady violinist, a couple of nylon-string classical guitarists in traditional garb similar to lederhosen, with bold motif leather bibs covering their chests, and a man with a military style side-drum clattered the three and fours of the bars to indicate when to move one's feet. They easily twisted their fingers into strummy bar chords, moving forward for the pre-requisite classical solos. A guitarist and the violinist sung well rehearsed harmonies, honed over hundreds of dates in villages and fiestas traversing the country every summer, the cute melodies drifting across the balmy continental tableau. The girls turned and watched, older couples indulged, swaying romantic old-school waltzes in front of the twinkling stage. Young people started to gather, and a few groups of students, the lads, Vespas parked-up, on the margins, supping cokes and smoking, standing and sitting in café shop-fronts and outside. Food finished, the Sacred Hearts decamped to the open-air tables, the girls chatted incessantly, their legs tapping to the live music, ogling the boys, their hearts racing with sugar and youthful spirit. Alphonso and his flouty pavement position had attracted two town motorbike Carabinieri, fascist style hats and long black boots not deterring him. He fast-talked and gesticulated toward the divine-trio, highlighting their responsibility as guardians for a group of vulnerable single women. He passed fags, and they lit up, the police satiated, sloping off to find real crime. By this time, the guardian-triad were tapping their toes, and clapped to the beat-group, assisted by God's nectar, three full wine beakers on their tin table-top, and the square was filling up with many more visitors, families and friends, only just turned out from evening mass in the best livery. The schoolgirls doubled-partnered, emulating the quirky waltz, alternating hops and kicks, every verse. They got pulled, compelled by the rotating throng, and soaked into the hubbub.

I often dream of standing on the tall church cross towering over the Piazza de Repubblica that night, floating above the pilgrims, swirling jubilant multitude below, a whirlpool of connected humanity, shifting, synchronised. Knowing Elsbeth was there gives me a sense of peace, that the world is right, that everything is going to be fine, joyful people, casting problems aside, forgetting the toil, in the moment - it makes me so happy that my Mother was light, innocent, drowning in fun and love and freedom, a time before me, a time before ConeBoy.

The moon was full, air electric. Every rotation, the girls came back into view, Alphonso observed, the nuns waved, slapping their palms together in tempo. A dozen boys located on the other side, hanging side-stage, knowing one of the bands, smiled as the strangers went by, innocently waving, not knowing what to make of the tourists. The girls had seen them, played up as they passed, making little shimmies, ignoring them on purpose. The young-men anyway. The two were one, close, slow-dancing, his arms encasing her trim waist, hers exploring his spine to his coccyx, swaying gently, the Popsters feet away, strumming the familiar pop mantra of a million darkened dancehalls. Cheeks brushed, lips brushed, he could feel her nubile nipples like bullets, erect against his, through his dusky shirt. Now the other girls weren't there, Elsbeth had been glided off, slow-danced toward the palazzo undercover walkway that cornered the marketplace, small shadowy shop-fronts, doorways, and corsia running behind shading doric pillars. She didn't resist. He pressed his leg between her womanhood, hers parted, Elsbeth's buttocks hard against the cold pillar, her eyes closed, juices flowed between them, intractable linking. Saliva swirled, intoxicating, meshed, lives weaved, land and sea that separated them Moses-miracled. She ran her palm to the nape of his neck her tongue flicked, diamond encrusted behemoth pierced her platinum ring. A wild judder engulfed her, and the band clattered into 'House of The Rising Sun'.

Smocks flew, panic, hearts hard beating, heavens quaked. Intoxicants vapourised by fear and adrenalin. The sacred-triad were sick, pulling out the girls they could see, crossing back-and-forth, crossing over, re-crossing, counting, re-counting, pointlessly counting, the students bemused, confused, embarrassed, a spectacle. There was no emergency phone, no contingency, hyped on wits, witless, competency thrown to the wind, hand-written risk assessments, and parent consent forms braising a hole in a metal filing cabinet somewhere back in the United Kingdom. The combo kept bearing down, sound reverberating off thick dry portal walls, noise previously celebratory now a sour roar that engulfed the holy-bunch nerves, and prevented rounding up their charges. Alphoso took the guilt, he'd known what boys could be, here, or anywhere, he'd taken his eye off the ball. It wasn't his job, he was a driver, but he took it, such was his personality. It was a first, he'd never lost a soul before.

Django was released without charge. He was sullen and irreverent to the Police, they knew him already, minor weed misdemeanours, perhaps a result of itinerant closely related parents having abandoned him to Grandparents. They'd respectably sweet-talked the mayor for leniency at the time, his artistic merits brandished as a benefit to the town. The two inveterate

constabulary-men couldn't wait to get him out of their cells after an

endless night of hysteria and goading from the spooked saintly-ones.

They, being God's wives, couldn't wait to blame someone else. The

girls sat bored, tired, and cold, in the unheated stony vestibule of the

Montaione Stazione, the environs more suited to drunken

overnighters, and petty thieves. Mafia kept the peace anyway. The

eleven girls who'd been whooping it up minus the assistance of local

yobs were eventually allowed to change, put on warm clothes, and

tromp back to the mini-bus, with Alphonso, who'd given a

purposeless written statement to the policemen. Zilch had happened,

no law breach, or provable offence. Elsbeth sat stony, frightened,

introverted, elbows on her knees, questions rained on her. She had a

little blood on her panties, and each time a nun started softly, another

jutted in, becoming more frustrated, none comprehending how to

handle the situation, no experience, no training, no precedent. Was

it rape and how to ask what they daren't express themselves; penis,

cock, phallus, member, labia, hymen, clitoris, vagina. Had she seen

it? Had it gone inside her? Had he put his fingers near private

parts? The night dragged on, and the police at long last drew it to a close, their findings a pile of nebulosity. The seventeen arrived at the hotel two hours before they had to leave for the airport. Phone calls were made, the embassy informed. Elsbeth was now a pariah, the rest of the girls either jealous, resentful, or angry. Suzi and Amanda felt culpable, and were perplexed.

Elsbeth found an inner resilience, she was contented, even exhilarated, a convert, she'd fallen in love. A secret scrap of course art-paper was tucked in her compact culottes' pocket, unseen by the saintly-accusers, and gendarmerie. Django had torn a corner from his tiny scribble notebook - that which contained heaps of colour swatches, daubs, creative ticks and obsessive inspired doodling - pushed deep inside his 501's back pocket, next to two stubby pencils, HB, and 3H. He'd quickly scrawled his address and phone number, virtually impossible to read, under no condition expecting to hear from this elusive angel ever again, then the shit-storm had poured, Alphoso and the two policemen roughing him away from Elsbeth, startling her, him, both victims and accused, wrapped into one. Amanda and Suzi, still larking with the remainder of the boys, had been violently screamed at, "Elsbeth, where's Elsbeth!" they indicated toward the general area, stunned, ashamed, recoiling. Elsbeth covertly transferred the note into a hidden crevice of her valise, the whole party bathed, changed back into school-uniform, meticulously inspected by the Sisters, then headed for the airport, another driver, another bus, Alphonso suspended, relieved of duties, pending…….. Realistically, that was the end of his reputation and job. He was resigned to it. It was God's way. Just as the nuns had heaped blame on him, the policemen, the town, the country, the weather, the music, Elsbeth, her friends, and the ground that surroundeth them.

Mr. Alphonso went on the tanker trucks, heaving the olive oil to and fro, biting his lip at the mob's ubiquity. Men with slicked back hair, black shirts, and baseball bats guarded the outside of factories, works, transfer stations, building sites, the number of trucks and materials clocked in and out, chitties exchanged, legitimacy and criminality blurred. Tuscany functioned, little rocked or changed over hundreds of years. Phonelines were hot for a spell - the Embassy, Head of Police, luckless plods, town hall, mayor, and various other beagles dragged in to the affair - but they went cold, no-one had an appetite for criminalising a teenager for doing what teenagers are meant to do. Alphoso would drive up to the bodyguards, smile, pass over his carnet, drive off, and spit out the window into the dust, at them, cursing, unseen, un-heard. And so life continued, yet this time the earth had displaced off its axis a micro-millimetre.

Elsbeth arrived on English soil, not only to Bob the driver, but a plethora of concerned parents and botherers. Anyone would think the girls had been in an avalanche. The only avalanche had been the amount of steam generated by the incident, Sacred-Heart management, sub-management, Principles, Head, Deputy Head, Assistants to the Head and Deputy Head, County Counsellors, Unions, Parent Association, Friends of Sacred Hearts, Alumni, Insurers, School Inspectors, Police, Uncle Tom Cobley, and half of them were at the airport to meet the disgraced. It was mandatory for the local pre-teens, on the council estates, and in the state schools to have a feel-up behind the bike sheds, and at the youth-club disco the last Sunday of every month. It was sex-education, coming-of-age, defining margins, experimental, having a laugh, yet, for this set it was mortifying moral debasement. Elsbeth's problem was, she got caught. The happenstance shaped her, as she couldn't really see what she'd done wrong, and refused the guilt. Her outlook metamorphosed. No longer the innocent excitable child, wholly involved, she'd become the onlooker, the observer, an outsider. The system started to strangle, and between fifteen and sixteen a vast change happened. My conception got closer.

CHAPTER 5 - BOBBY DYLAN

Gash is animated, "Chuck it on man, don't be fuckin' shy with it."

Django is wrestling with paint and brushes that seem like big breeze

blocks in his formerly skilful flairish grip. Before skag, paint would

have flung itself magically from the brushes in flourishes, landing

where intended. Even Gash knows it's amateurish, and he'd only

ever experienced art in a vain attempt by his school to drag an

insolent hostile bunch of Stockport teenagers round Manchester Art

Gallery.

"What do you know, you can't even play guitar."

Django is frustrated and reddening.

"I play better than you fuckin' paint you fuckin' washed up wop."

Django precociously throws the whole pot across the canvas, blue

splashing in a great mountain, soaking over the yellow he'd already

carefully laid on it, and beyond onto the floor. "The floor needed

fuckin' painting anyway you daft cunt."

Gash maddens Django even more and chucks his roll-up fag end,

neatly smoking onto the evolving creation, and takes a swig from his

pale ale can. The paint puts it out, a brisk hissing sound.

"I tell you what, I'll play you a nice tune if you paint me a pretty picture," Gash speaking hardly as the can has left his lips, still butted up against the brim of his Nazi hat, his long jewish nose almost blocks his gulping. Gash sits with his pointing face bemused, jet black jeans, across a couple of cushions, the only furnishings to have graced chez-Djangos, an equally black, size small, Siouxsie and the Banshees t-shirt, rifled from a merchandiser's box backstage on a European gigging outpost. A two-inch distressed black leather belt is so tight, the twenty-seven inch waisted jeans are easily mistaken for twenty-six or twenty-five. The legs taper so narrow that they tail off in protest into the ankles of his Cuban heels. Bought on Carnaby Street, the boots are black and white two-tone, with two-inch heels that extend Gash's gaunt frame, essential when confronting irate German artic drivers. Gash has learned to load heavy drums and amplifiers into venues toppling on these stilts. His right hand jean pocket bulges, rectangular, with a tobacco box, which he reaches for, with two fingers. He can only get two fingers in the space between box and material, the jeans badly worn here. He has to stretch out a leg to gain sufficient finger momentum to get any grip on the tinwear. Gash removes the lid, places it upturned on the floor, and puts the box inside. It fits snugly. He tidies it. It's in sections, a drug Tardis. As well as housing his tobacco, there's uppers of various pigment and trait, like mini-Anadins, separated neatly by homemade cardboard partitions. He swallows a couple of uppers, takes another guzzle of beer, as Django is removing his clothes. "What you fuckin doin' man?" Gash leers up amused, from his rolling-up duty. He lights up, the untidy fibres at the end burning bright red and fizzling out immediately, then takes his bashed-up acoustic, fag in mouth, and starts on Bob Dylan's 'Like A Rolling Stone'. He rams out the E and G chords ineptly, but his croaking voice suits the rendition, his northern boy splatter adding zip. Django is putting on a strip show, neatly folding each item of clothing on his and Elsbeth's mattress. He hadn't folded a piece of clothing in his life, so it's hysterical to Gash, who snorts through "How does it feel, to be without a home." Django's in his underpants, brown, then bright blue because he's spread-out, rolling on the canvas, which takes in his full height and width as he straddles it covering himself in oils, his black hair now electric blue. Gash reverses the cushion with his bum, out of the line of fire, avoiding the paint dots gunning off the handiwork.

"Knock knock knocking on heaven's door, Django's rolling on the floor." Django lays on his tummy forming a snow angel, his head on its side staring in the other direction from Gash, threshing his arms like flying, to make shapes. Gash lays the guitar on the floor beside him face up, taking red carefully, so as not to get it on his shoes, and pours it on to Django, so it lunks down his spine.

"Now you're talkin' man, it looks like something."

Django feels the cold paint on his back, rolls over to spoil the pure blue and yellow mass, and the red bleeds in. Django kneels, dabbing and pumping it with his fist, and volcanoes of colour spit up, and fall back on to the canvas randomly.

"That's it man, don't spoil it, that's enough! Djangy, that's enough man!"

Django thumps the canvas repeatedly, dents it, possessed, deranged, crying his heart out. "She's not coming back is she, she's not coming back." His tears drop into paint, insignificant, salty water peeling off the oil, fleeting. Django recoils into foetal position, head held by his discoloured hands, "I hate that fuckin' baby, that fuckin' unborn, I'll lose Elsbeth, my Elsbeth, she's not coming back." Gash stunned, iced, roll-up burning close to his strained lips, pot in one hand, the other caught, static, mid-air, tart cherry stains his white

heels.

CHAPTER 6 - PINE HILL, FILLYWOOD

Elsbeth's case, with the coloured stripes circumnavigating it sits upended on the stairs, propped on the fourth thickly carpeted step. It's her ancient school case, the leather and her embroidered name tag now battered and grimy, where dust that had built up at St. Peter's Grove is ingrained. It had sat in the corner of her and Django's flat, a storage utility punters would handily sit on, as there was no furniture. Made to withstand a Tsunami, in one of Britain's finest tanneries, she'd take it to her grave. The single item she carried with her, arriving at Ladroke Grove twelve years ago. It was home, where it had first been used, on the Florence trip, or D-Day as her father referred to it. He eyed the case, but remained mute. He'd walked past it on his way to the kitchen from the dining room, but wouldn't take it up to Elsbeth's old room. That was a step too far. The hallway is as big as some council houses on the other side of Woking, where the overflow estates stretch out, separating from the town, invisible to visitors and the genteel middle-classes, who frequent the upmarket shops in the town centre, and splurge onto early non-stop commuter trains to London. It carries through the main Tudor theme of the downstairs at Pine Hill, Fillywood Lane. Deep oak floors, panelled walls, carved wood detail, light rugs, expensive paintings and pottery. Bits Eileen had collected for many years, from holidays, antique shops. It reads comfort, and exclusivity. Plumbing, lighting, bathrooms, and kitchen had been sympathetically up-dated, William and Eileen filling their time instructing local builders and contractors, when they should have been attending school plays, passing outs, award ceremonies, swimming galas, sports days, university induction days, graduations, family holidays, engagement parties, a wedding, wedding reception, marquee band and catering hired for the grounds, birthday celebrations, Christmases, christenings, and baptisms. It's a long walk from the dining room to the kitchen, past the stairwell, which leads up to a balcony, splitting the upstairs into two, both with their own reception hall and banisters, where one can review proceedings below like an Elizabethan farce. William had plenty of time to consider the valise before reaching the kitchen, and back out to the gardens, staring at it, memories staking his brain like pointed cleft chestnut posts.

"Bring your case, I'll show you to your room." Eileen returns to the dining room, having cleared the crockery after pudding, and collects Elsbeth.

"I know where my room is thank you Mummy."

Regardless, Eileen proceeds. It's hushed, they cross the hall, the half dozen or so steps like walking a tightrope for Eileen. She'd prayed for this day so many times, for so many years, now it was here, it lacked significance. It's mundane. Elsbeth's floating hippy attire, bracelets and necklaces swish, clank, jangle, like a big percussion bell-tree, too powerful in the subdued atmosphere.

"We couldn't decide whether to put you in your old room, it's a bit old-fashioned compared with the others, we had en-suites done, except in yours, then you've your own bathroom anyway, at the end of your hall, so it makes no odds, and your father said…" Eileen had started to ramble edgily, and Elsbeth gingerly interrupts, "It's okay, I realise it's difficult, sorry, I wouldn't have asked had I not…"

Eileen, on the fifth step, stops abruptly, twisting her top half, facing Elsbeth who's bent, righting her case, to pick it up, bracelets racing to meet her wrist, only to be tugged back up again, the same movement repeated forty times a day. The toe of Eileen's brogue clanks against the Victorian brass stair rod. "You'll have to relieve yourself of some of the arm furniture darling, sorry, sorry, you know what your Dad is like." Elsbeth is surprised but not perturbed by the awkwardness and slight rudeness of her mother, "Yes, of course, I'm sorry Mummy."

"Not much has changed, we thought of decorating it, but know you liked it, it does get cleaned, we didn't lock it up, thinking you'd never be back, the cleaner does do it, it's not the same lady, you probably don't remember, Gladys died, we paid for her funeral as it goes, a lovely one, out at Aldershot Crematorium, she'd been with us, oh, since we'd been here, seen her kids go to school, even put a pot toward their uni' funds, who'd think, you wouldn't get loyalty like that now, what with Thatcher, it's all me me me, even your father dislikes her, and he's about as conservative as they come." They arrive at the door. Elsbeth and Eileen stand next to each other, trepidatious. "Well go ahead, it's your home," Eileen's voice crackling. Elsbeth rotates the brass handle and pushes the door wide open, dolls line walls, posters of The Kinks, Gerry and the Pacemakers, Beatles, Jesus, her silver cross necklace hangs from the wooden handle of her bedside table, on which sits a silver desk lamp, from a slaughtered pig.

Brightness so hard I may as well been on the surface of the sun, a cold cruel sun, warmth sloshed asunder, onto the filthy floor. Gagging for clean air, to breathe, to gorge the hellish smelling rough oxygen, lungs saturated, umbilical cut, pain bit. I'm gasping, saturation cauterised into my brain, the burning memory of gasping for life. Gagging, I was sucking on my own mulch, pulling on my fleshy facial labia, slurping up my disorder, rasping for breath, chronic fresh-air divides me from life. A cake of facial bone, skeletal weave-work crusted sinew and distorted lattice work crushing life from me. I'm dying, thank God. Star of wonder, Star of night, Star with royal beauty bright, Westward leading, still proceeding, Guide us to the perfect light.

"Kill it, fuckin' kill it!"
"Give me the fuckin' thing!"
"Arggghhh, what is that, fuckin' Jesus Christ, it's fuckin' head."
"Call an ambulance!"
"Get down to the phone box and call a fuckin' ambulance."

"999, dial 999!"

Kate's screaming, then pukes violently, kneeling, her pink jeans rip more at the knees as she scrapes away from the sight, guffing up food which she didn't know existed in her gut. Only Tasleen has a check on reality, her hands shaking violently cupping the specimen over Elsbeth's motionless body, holding it as far away as possible without actually dropping it, as if it's a piece of dog-crap she's had to pick up with her bare hands, in her own kitchen, and dump in the bin. Ramona has her back against the door, wishing it would suck her through, without having to open it first. She cannot avert from the disaster unfolding, like the family car turned over on the icy slip-road, in deep north London fog - as she glares from the back of a punk group's van drodging up the M1, for another futile northern gig - the family inside mashed up by a jack-knifed Scottish neeps truck, all blood and loss. Ramona's perky skin tone has drained, she's pinned like Jesus tied to the cross, awaiting stigmata. Gash levers the door, her, and clatters himself down the stairs, desperately hoping the public phone hasn't been vandalised for small change. He'd been a cat-on-hot-coals, the smoking ban, dolphins bleating on the stereo, contraction screams and hours spent helping friends with home-labour wasn't his cup-of-tea. The head disfigurement hadn't phased him, a year in a Rochdale slaughterhouse after leaving school at fifteen dulled squeamishness. If the phone box was out-of-order, he already had plan-B. Elsbeth has passed out. Physical pain seared her pelvis and tore into her back, overpowering her drug-weakened body, which was completely un-prepared for birthing. She saw the legs pulled out totally normal, and as the head appeared she fainted. Limbs akimbo straddling the makeshift birthing-pool, most of the warm water it had been filled with is gone, plans awry. Elsbeth has splashed out the entire contents onto Ali, Tasleen and Johnno, Django, the punkettes and Gash. It has extinguished the dozens of candles placed in careful configurations about the kiddie's paddling-pool, and room. Now a lone bare bulb above lights the four remaining, surrounding the recent mother.

"Cut the cord, cut it," Tasleen instructs Johnno, his shaking black hands covered in bodily fluids, milky mucus with tiny clotted blood pustules exploding as he bravely manipulates the membrane, like one of the greasy pitch-covered London double-decker brake hoses he works on. He's mechanically adept, averting scrutiny of the baby's head. Ali is holding Elsbeth's head slightly up on his knees, he's taken over from the deflated rim of the rubber-ring which acted as a pillow. It's his one task, he's carrying it out despite having been glued there for an hour, soaking wet, and in shock. Only Django can see close up, he is leaning right over Elsbeth and the baby, listening. "It's not breathing, it's gasping for breath Tas," he says quietly, the bedlam and shock around him blinkered out.

"I don't know Djan', I just don't know, it needs a doctor, the placenta has to come out, she has to push it out."

Django stares right into the infant's face, the alien flaps, knitted woven riven seams of crusted membranous baggage girdle the misshapen eyes, no perceivable mouth or nose, skin dangling, flaccid, there are internal blood vessels on show, human ducts.

"It's going to die, let it die Djan', let's concentrate on Elsbeth, she's not gonna make it," says Johnno, unusually forceful. Django looks up, and around, as if searching for a God-sent medical miracle from a practitioner's tool-box. The conical ice-cream cones sitting on the small draining board catch his eye, a box half opened, the ones so beloved by Elsbeth. A pregnancy craving, snacking, to compliment the cool soothing Lyons Maid ice cream, the only nutriment she'd digest in the last weeks.

"Ramona, the cones!"

Ramona is a rabbit in headlights.

"Ramona, get the ice-cream cones!!" Django screams. He looks to Ali, "Get the cones Ali." Ali looks up, "Take her head," in his imperceptibly clipped South African. Django pulls himself over, takes Elsbeth's head. Ali jumps up, rocks due to cramp, smoothes dripping wet hair off his face, and lugs himself over to the cone box, slipping on the soaked boards, nearly tripping on a large crystal. He steadies himself on the drainer, pulls the box off the top, and turns on the spot, taking the four steps back to Django, handing over the blue and yellow Walls box.

"What's happening Django, we don't have time for this?" Tasleen offers a little sensibility in the disaster-zone. "Take her head Ali," Django is uncharacteristically lucid, and Ali resumes his Elsbeth vigil, the woman of his dreams lying nude next to him, but not in the condition he'd necessarily fantasized. "She is breathing," exhales Ali, not realising his repetition.

"There's no breath, it's dying Django, there's nothing there to breathe with Django, let's give it up and help Elsbeth," insists Tasleen.

Ramona is slumped to the floor, crying, wailing, and Kate crawls toward her, wipes the phlegm and gunk from her chin and neck, and draws Ramona in with both arms. Kate's voice is hard and uncompromising, her American accent resurrected, that which had been replaced by mockney since she'd been brought to England age nine. "We have to go, we can't be here." Ramona and Kate's eyes connect, they'd never done so before, having been united in self-indulgence, or 'rebellion' as they liked to refer to it, they'd not in any way had real unity. "No, no," Ramona replies weakly, seeing right into Kate's soul. Kate uses all her strength to get Ramona half up, but Ramona is inconsolable, her voice burbly, "Beth's going, she could die, why, why didn't we do something." Kate's timbre is tough, won in previous hardship, "It's not for us...."

Django interrupts Ali's constant jabber, mellifluous, Mediterranean, powerful, "Leave her head, lay it, she'll be okay, I've seen her out-of-it man, hundreds of times, she'll come round, just get those two out, the girls." "OK, she's breathing." Django is drying out, the stress and concentration boiling every heat particle in his body, his hair has frizzed, and lacks the smooth habitual slick of

"Where did you get that at four in the morning?"

"There was chip van."

"Chip van?"

"Yeah, a fuckin' chip van man."

"You're joking."

"No?"

"I've never seen a chip van."

"Chepstow Villas, it was on Chepstow Villas."

"You've been all the way down to Chepstow Villas?"

"I legged it there, no phone boxes, ran all the way."

"A night van on Chepstow Villas?"

"Yeah, posh bastards."

"Will you two shut the fuck up about a chip van," snarls Tasleen.

Gash distributes the warm paper packages, the outer Daily Mirror newspaper wrapping already vinegarised. "Does mine have a saveloy?" pipes Johnno. Sirens come into audible range, slapping up Ladbroke Grove from Holland Park Avenue, the stillness of the spring night amplifying the top frequencies of the dee-dah dee-dah dee-dah. Gash interjects and runs out, enjoying the night-time spotlight, "I'm going to the end, get them to come up the right way." Light breaths pulse from Elsbeth's mouth, lids flickering. Johnno goes over to the window behind the mattress, and rasps back the drudgey curtain material covering the aperture. It's tough, stuck to the rail with ground in grime. He yanks and it breaks a little, but he's wrestled an opening, the street lights filtering in. He looks below, and addresses Elsbeth, his back to her, his words sincere, tar face sodium lit, they drop slowly from his tired thick lips, "They're here, the ambulance is here, you're going to hospital." What is invisible, under the duvet is the excessive bleeding, from between her legs. Johnno retreats, and the two godparents congregate with pater beneath the centre lightbulb, their calorie fatigued bodies are drained of any sense of responsibility or reality. Django breathes, "We did it, it's gonna be okay." At that instant the leaded light-catcher, revealed by the open drapes, is suddenly twirled by an excessive rush of air coming from the ground floor. A wave of emergency service personnel ascend the staircase, a clomping barrage balloon of regularity. They're a whirlwind, an eddy. The pentangle's unusual rotation allows it to catch a ray from the street arc, splintering the room. It shimmers a little, a fabricated welcoming warmth transforms the pigsty, the three dark strangers

immobile, parcels outstretched, see a radiance sparkling above the

crib, a halo touches the suckling-boy.

CHAPTER 8 - DIARRHOEA

"Only sixteen, only sixteen," two unburdened scrumpy shrill voices screech the Sam Cooke hit, the broad barley field and high summer crops protecting any neighbours from the girly rapture. Elsbeth and Michaela are searing songsters, cross-legged drop-out yoga'ey pose cherished by festival goers, and right-on gigging chicks. Bell bottoms, mini, crop-tops, beads, the full faddy gear, gearing up with a little gear of their own, a spliff, and somewhere to be. Michaela is eighteen, a trussed raven-haired skinny dope-smoking beautiful hippy. She met Elsbeth, 'Elsie', at a Small Faces gig at Guildford Civic Hall, a regular Home Counties stop off for ensembles worming their way back south to London or Brighton. The place was often half-full, and it mattered not, since the Borough Arts committee were forward thinking, funding classical, jazz and R&B. William and Eileen had dropped her off, as she was meeting school pal Amanda. Elsbeth ditched the sporty pair months back, and had quickly slipped into the toilets to change. She wasn't the only counties girl with the same intent. She had emerged in bastardised flowery print dress, cut just below her crotch, velvet choker, a slim black head band from which locks floated, weaved from cherubs' wings - or so it seemed -

as she broke hearts walking through the room. The Bracknell Hells

Angel chapter, who had a squalid squat above the Virginian Café in

Camberley, had requisitioned the bar, other drinkers timidly edging

them for frothing pints of Watney's. The police wouldn't go near, it

was more trouble. A pair of elderly St. John's Ambulance

volunteers, who doubled as makeshift invigilators, were hopelessly

out-gunned, and the hall staff looked more like ABC cinema

confectionary sellers than concert organisers. Marriot's management

had seen it all before, one of their road managers came out, un-

phased, sorting protection money amongst the thugs. That's exactly

what the Angels wanted, a skim, to look menacing, and so they did.

Later, they bunched side stage, sulkily nodding-dog for the duration

of the band's set, glaring over the crowd. Marriot didn't care, he

made the same spitting invective into the punters, Guildford,

Aberdeen, Middlesbrough, Swansea, Minsk, it amounted to the

same, music, drink, speed, girls. More than one biker chatted her up,

their armour-plating melting into submission at her perfectly formed

lips, and dusky eye-shadowed lids that fluttered at their dim rocker

lines. She could have wafted a kiss and they would have fallen backwards on their chain bike belts, and greasy leather waistcoats. When she flitted off, every boy's eyes ogled her progress through the sweaty packed throng. Elsbeth stood at the back rocking back and forth to the northern support act, who were pumping out plagiarised Hendrixy riffs, a hint of English progressive seeping through, wah-wah wafting from the fifteen inch bass bins, psychedelic lighting and oil wheel projections. The Small Faces attracted an odd combination of teenyboppers, and serious music fans, Steve Marriot's chimpy looks juxtapositioning muscular soul scream and chopping Epiphone six-string, bridging both camps. It was easy to see how, not long after, he'd be on the road with prototype mettalers Humble Pie.

Meeting was seamless, they looked almost the same. In a small community it was easy to be attracted to similar, Michaela asking Elsbeth for a light. Elsbeth didn't have one, but by the end of the night she'd become 'Elsie', had smoked dope at Michaela's tiny bedsit at the top of Bridge Street, and listened in full stereo to The Doors, Frank Zappa, and The Nice. Elsie belonged. The police picked her up on Clay Lane at 3 am, between Guildford and Woking, walking home. William had been out, driving for hours, reluctant to call the police again, but badgered by Eileen into submission, having bisected the long deserted market-town streets, university campus, in the gloom of the cathedral, sadly lit with sodium street lamps, his headlamps illuminating a bunch of zip, a terrified knot in his abdomen. They didn't say much, glad to have her home again. A sheen of normality in the morning, dissent from Elsbeth now pervading their everyday norms. William in his city togs, and Eileen getting Elsbeth up for school.

Out in the fields the prog-pals have swigged the apple ferment, and are hoping for more thrills, a complete day of bunking responsibility ahead of them, to celebrate Elsie's coming-of-age. Michaela is a copy-clerk at Winters' Publishers, a grand name for a modest bi-monthly set of periodicals that service the Butcher and Grocery trades. She'd gone there straight out of school, to the stuffy hammerbeamed first floor offices at the crest of North Street. Her passport was a couple of Guildford High School English O levels, combined with a pleasingly eager demeanour, which concealed laziness and manipulation. Michaela harboured dreams for the music business, yet held no skill, qualification, or ambition. They'd advertised it as a journalistic opportunity. It wasn't. She would eventually, at thirty, through pal of a pal, procure a receptionist job at the Rough Trade record warehouse that bordered the rear of scuzzy King's Cross. In the disordered chaos she'd answer phones, put calls through, see managers and pluggers in, get to see bands for free, and snap up new records, pre-release. She got a flat sharing with the guitarist from 'Slaughter and The Dogs' just off Chiswick High Road, and was, in her mind, living the dream. Her dive was the pub nearby, on Devonshire Road, which had one of the first Space Invaders machines in London. Thus, it became the preferred weekday hang-around for bands like The Members, and The Hammersmith Gorillas, fingers thumping big black buttons, a crew of onlookers awaiting their turn, downing hyper-addictive super-strong pints of IPA. She bedded the right man, as the advantage she'd held with looks had started to wane. He got out of punk rock when the majors started releasing synthesiser bands, and opened a shoe shop across the road with her, she being the gregarious front, and he the business mind and stimuli.

"Let's go to my place," Elsie pipes, slurred, and beady-eyeing Michalea to get her grip. Michaela summons, sing-songey like a nursery rhyme, "Your Mummy will be home." Elsie knows, putting on her poshest Queen, imitating her mother, "Not today, it's golf, lunch at the club." They both pause, Elsie twiddling a broken barley stalk, "They won't miss a couple of bottles of brandy, I'm always taking swigs."

"Okay Elsie, be it on you."

"I can hear the car pull up anyway, we can bunk across the garden into the stables, I've done it loads of times."

"Okay, let's go."

"It'll be fun, I can show you *my* records."

It's a short walk from Brooklands, which is midway between Sacred Heart and Fillywood Lane, where the two often meet. They're an unusual sight on the lanes. There isn't a lot of activity on a workday afternoon. Elsbeth can't walk quite straight, and they hold arms drunkenly falling about, in fits of absurdity. They halt at a bus-stop shelter seat, and are propositioned by a couple of drivers, who slowly pull over. The girls snicker, taking the piss out of the puzzled leerers. They start up again, Michaela piping in, "You told me, dimwitty, he's coming in a month."

"Shitty dimwitty, you're shitty dim-wittey pretty little shitty," Elsie daftly prodding her polished fingernail at Michaela.

"Yes, Django lovely Django Biancho, Django, Django Bianchoooo, the man of my dreams. You know….. Anyway… you open all his letters before you give them to me!"

Elsie trips.

"Only as quality control," and both fall about in hysterics, Michaela pulling Elsie, red hipster flares flapping.

"I AM quality control officer!" Michaela does her robotic voice.

"I phoned him anyway."

"Phoned?"

"I spoke some Italian, and he spoke some English, and he said he loves me."

They walk, talk, breathless, a motorcyclist goes by, sounds his horn, a shrill beep making them jump, and they stick two fingers up at him. He glances in his rear mirror and Churchill's them back.

"A year at St. Martin's, I think it's a scholarship, um…, I didn't really understand."

"You won't like him, after all he's got fat, fat arse lardy fat eating too much pasta fat."

straight to the sink stand, dousing her mouth underneath the cold tap, spluttering, "This is bigger than my whole flat," holding back her hair, wiping her lips like a miner on his lunch break. Elsie gets glasses out of the vintage clapperboard cupboard above her head, tops them up at the tap and drinks hers, goes to the fridge for food, takes out cheddar cheese, then a loaf from the bread bin, opens the butter dish and makes sandwiches.

"Pickle?"

"Where's the brandy?" Michaela, no interest in food. Elsie carries on, flicks her head to the double doors, "Second on the left after the stairs, in the drinks cabinet, don't touch the expensive stuff, they'll know. Bring it with you, I've ice and coke." Michaela has regained her confidence, and floats across the reception perusing the walls, paintings, family pictures, lots of Elsie as a baby and toddler, in a woolly hat bouncing in snow, on a sledge, school shots, a family portrait, the Henderson's in oils. She stops, studies the painting, sliding her finger around the deeply inlaid frame, pedestrian, contemplating, buried flashes of her own childhood flicker in her mind, she nods in the negative and tuts instinctively. She rolls down the frame to a golf club leaned at the base of the stairs, propped in-between the banister and wall, so it won't fall, the dirtied stainless steel base is stamped with a large five.

"Rum, I fancied rum," Michaela bursts, drinking straight out the bottle.

"Shute, hadn't thought of that, there's lemonade," Elsie pings to the utility room and finding the White's bottle, fizzing the top undone, glugs it into the emptied water glasses. They both sit up on the breakfast stools, either side of the central reservation, consuming cheese and pickle wedges, with rum and lemonade, the rum portions overly generous. They stare at each-other like lovers, attempting big-eye-balling in a who-will-laugh-first game, Elsie losing.

"Come up and look at my records."

Michaela pushes a piece of cheese, orbiting her plate, "Hmmm, no, let's go, another time." Elsie pleads, "Oh, come on, no-one will be back for hours, we can go in the pool."

"I don't........ What's that?!"

Michaela looks to the upstairs, even though she is just viewing the ceiling. They're taken aback by the clunk. Elsie finishes her hunk and belts the drink, she is again feeling how she wants, numbed. Michaela is still looking up, concerned, then looks at Elsie.

"It's just, it's your place, I'm not used to it, let's take the rum and go, we can get the bus back in to town, there was a stop." Elsie looks over Michaela's shoulder at the mains kitchen wall clock, big clear black hands against white face, "The bus is ten past the hour, we just missed one, let's just hang around until then, c'mon Michaela, please?" Michaela drops her head, and there's another creak from the ceiling direction.

"Alright, but you better not have ghosts, this place gives me the creeps, if I'm honest."

Elsie slips off the seat, "The house makes noises, it's ancient." Slickly, she clears the mess, wiping the top, gliding behind Michaela, putting on a hushed demonic voice right by her ear, "Yeah, ghosts, there's ghosts, I'm going to kill you and feed you to the ghosteyyyyy's." Michaela jumps and slaps her, "Don't, you shit," and they guffaw.

"Bring the bottle," Elsie says, and they leave, trailing upstairs, their brown long boots thucking against the deep pile strips covering the treads. Elsie reaches the brow of the stairs, Michaela two behind. There's a thump. "What! I'm going!" Michaela voices, clutches at Elsie's skirt from behind. "Shh," Elsie turns and concentrates her pupils on Michaela who still holds the skirt, liquor dispensed with, the other hand grips the banister, like she could fall. Elsie puts her finger, long, slender, slowly to her mouth, "Shhh!…. It's burglars, give me the bottle, you go to the phone, it's in the office, call the police." Michaela's glued, terrified, her clench has started to shudder, she just about mouths, "No, I'm staying with you." Elsie retrieves the drink, begins to move, to the left, the opposite direction to her bedroom, where the sound is, screwing the rum cap tight, raising the bottle, ready to make a stand. There's the thump, louder, then more, there are two at a time, then three. They cease. The balcony becomes corridor, it's dingy, no windows, heavy period oak doors either side, a bathroom, guest room. Michaela points to the master bedroom, the door that frames the end of the passage. Under her breath, "It's there, coming from there, Mummy's jewellery." She signals for Michaela to follow her, on the other side, and they creep together hugging the walls. "Take the vase," Elsie motions to Michaela with her lips, again, "take the vase!" Michaela comes to her senses and takes the vase off of the bureau, it's a quarter her height, and she manoeuvres it so it can be gripped by the neck. They skulk more, step by step, and Michaela starts to cry, silently, tears streaming, her mascara Halloweening her face. Thudding resumes, it's regular. They are at the port, the harbour, ready to launch, set sail, cast-off, weigh anchor, put to sea, tallyho,

"GO!"

Elsie flings the black bolt studded door, and the twin-set banshee their way into the room, weapons cocked. Graham Stanley is stoking Eileen Henderson from behind, she bent, arched over the dressing table, furniture thwacks one last time, his erect penis involuntarily enters on its final outing, as his head crows towards the ingress, Eileen already knows what it is, her head locked. The vase splinters on the waxed tongue-in-groove, slow-motioning from Michaela's hand. Michaela is transfixed by the décor, a reliance on brown, and it's all she would be able to conjure from the incident for many years, one wall predominating, a miasma of orange and diarrhoea sludgy swirls. Eileen takes the penis, and pulls it out of her, handing it back to Graham Stanley like she's returning a badly stitched brassiere to Marks and Spencers. "It's alright darling, it's not what you think," Eileen's black stockings, suspenders, black gloss high-heels, breasts partly exposed, forced over her black lace girdle, Chanel top rasped partly off her arms, lose significance rapidly - her maternal instinct smelling up the room, replacing the sex aura. She seamlessly pops her breasts in, re-dons the trim, buttoning, like it hadn't been ripped from her in a lust frenzy, as she legs toward her daughter. Eileen addresses Michaela direct, cutting the aftermath, "And who are you, in my house in the middle of the day, you're the one are you, that's been leading Elsbeth astray, well you can bloody well get out now, and stay away from my daughter!" the controlled tone rising through the sentence, as it dawns on her their motives. Elsbeth throws the bottle sharp at Graham Stanley, and he is too stunned to duck, it circles, a high flying Red Kite, scorching rapier, Spitfire looping the loop over Salisbury Plain dipping behind a Messerschmitt for the final heroic rat-tat. Elsbeth's private dance lessons bear fruit, her pirouette giving her several seconds head-start, before her mother has traction in stilettos.

CHAPTER 9 - BEVIN

Smudges of spinning cyan flip off sepia'd brickwork, commotion, action, supervision, establishment, beacons' signalling, arrival, departure, reaction, solution, stuff is happening at The Grove, over here, have a gander, ogle, knock yourself out, bearing witness, at last there's occurrence, all change, after all, here's the wreckage, over there, have a look.

Flourishes of navy epaulettes, silver threading, London Ambulance Service, light-blue short-sleeved shirts, ironed arm creases, with slight turn-backs, pressed, two front pockets, containing only a pen, flint-blue tie, functional silver tie clip, gloomy slate trousers, one inch ironed turn-ups, a leather tiered triple pocket-bag clipped to a rear-belt loop, for scissors, sterile bandage, safety pins, assorted plasters.

"Bloomsbury 3, Bloomsbury 3, come in Bloomsbury 3." The two-way Motorola VHF AM radio nasal nagging in the empty thinly lit cab, both sliding front doors of the breadbox Bedford wide open, vacated in haste. Driver and passenger seeing to it, a duty, a task, a job, one they'd hope they wouldn't, one hour to go on their shift and it would have been a different unfortunate soul. Two men, one a twenty year old raw recruit, six constables, three Panda cars, bedlam, it is almost light, the birds are starting to wake, shouting their territorial joy all over the shop-of-horrors. The clasp of conjoined people finally disgorges from No.10, a C90 cassette propelled from an Amstrad deck, compilation tape, dissimilar tracks cleverly spliced together for a seamless apogee of moods. David Bowie, everyone likes him, Joy Division, not so sure, but it's only a minute until The Electric Light Orchestra and Abba.

The Police = authority - order - law - government - royalty - the Queen, God Save Her.

The Ambulance Service = healthcare - altruism - Bevin - community - Labour - Unions, Don't Get Me I'm Part of It.

Hippies = drop out - counterculture - drugs - freedom - eastern philosophy, Sexy Sadie, what have you done, you've made a fool of everyone.

Punk = nothing - nowhere - lost generation - DIY - working class - nihilist, We don't care about long hair, I don't wear flares.

Symbiotically emerging, a hunk of bodies, bizarre maelstrom, not slowly, but with real determination, concentration intense, each assigned their task, same intent, buddies, with a reason, a common goal, purposely, first aiders, father and the accomplishment of his loins, godfather, friends.

A fair audience has congregated for the hour at the base of the steps, gathering essential information for later, in nightclothes, or outdoorsy wear, thrown on. Most know Django, Elsbeth, Johnno, Tasleen, Gash, and the shock is palpable. Gossip is flowing, unknown piquing the furtive. It doesn't take much to part a way for the baby-grabbers, the alliance transmit a powerful solemnity that touches everyone. An alley forms either side of the gate brick pillars, the trainee's face is bleached of colour, with the horrendous task of attending to the catastrophe-child.

I have the urge to puke, nuke my guts, if it isn't bad enough being underdeveloped, having a head like treaded excrement in a lay-by, and breathing through a kiddie's seaside wafer pacifier. I needed smack, strong opiate injected direct into a festering scab on my arm, re-using a reliable elbow crease hole, tourniquet bloody dirty shoelace, needle and the spoon, black-hole sun, golden brown, brown sugar, I am waiting for my man, but he doesn't come. Only this gaggle of incompetent numbskulls. It turns on a sixpence, the drugs hit, warm glow, giddy, it is coursing my miniscule vessels, charabanc, convoy, cavalcade, whooping it up in my vein, a missile to the brain. Chronic comedown is averted, and I see the moths fluttering, spiralling the battery-draining strip lights in the ambulance back-box, I look up, my Daddy staring at me, I bond, three junkies, Mummy upstairs, Daddy, child together, my gilded carriage arrived.

Sliding night to day, and steadily-revolving police belishas drain reds from the buildings, casting a disconnected corrosion across St. Peter's. An hour not normally navigated by tenants of these parts adds to the peculiar fragile atmosphere. It could be Midnight Mass. Praying at the of ambulance altar, the flock hum in low voices, hushed tones, enter the Eternal Magus. Neon bulbs explode, reverence shatters, the group scatter with a bolt, an awakening, intruder's peep-hole, a black Nikon SLR thirty-five millimetre flicks off flash cartridges startling Django, Ambulance-rookie and the two policemen. Kate pushes up into the metallic manger, Ali behind her, and a man, intense, wide lens glued to his glasses. Bulbous paunch bloats a tight tattered anorak, a rip at the side revealing fleecy nylon lining. His trousers, of no style or form, sit beneath his gut, an unavoidably exposed bit of pork-belly revealed. The thin brown belt pulled in tight only accentuates it. Flaxen flopping hair ages him beyond his thirtyish slot, a chubby greasy face, morning stubble in control. Low grade paparazzi'ist has a large bobble nose, the rounding mainly at the tip. He's eyeless, sight formed of fifty millimetre, wide-angle, long-range, macro, telephoto, a world interpreted through hard Japanese polycarbonate and polished German glass. If one could see his eyes they'd be piggy, tired, bags below. Access all areas, camera the passport, suddenly his name's on the list - he's in, and got the shot. Exposures exhausted, he rolls the bulging resinous camera bag to his front, fast, automatic slicing. Nimbly releasing a side pocket press-stud, simultaneously rewinding the camera spool, he pulls the release and drops the film out, jointly replacing it with one from the bag. The whole exchange takes no longer than ten seconds, the exposed cartridge is slid to Kate and she explodes from the tailgate, stuffing it in her pocket, and hits the ground running, shouldering Ali out of the way. Ali has a combine-harvester in his pupils, chaffing, beating, slashing, scythes desiccating his rabid mind. He's not felt so confused, even when his father told him he was being sent to London. Lonely, damned, his existence has just bottomed out. Exhaustion, shock, and Kate's forceful driving enthusiasm, for what now dawns as an idiotic idea, suppurating logical reasoning.

"I want that film!" booms Django, standing. Ali hots it after Kate, but she's gone, turned the corner. The two policemen wake up to what's happening, the affair somewhat beyond their normal routine, they're discombobulated. The cameraman is forcibly helped from the ambulance, but he's still circling, clicking off the roll. Technically there's no crime being committed. They have other things to deal with, namely, saving ConeBoy and Elsbeth. The crowd cotton on, and he's jostled. He's steady, practised in the click-and-leave. He reverses, camera lowered adeptly into its case, beliefs. It suited her, and like the casualties coasting roundabout Ashbury Heights, the dream was long-gone, replaced by burnt out brain cells fried with LSD and heroin. Elsbeth sighs a long sigh, palms spread on the sill, tipping further toward the dormer.

Outside the autumn half-caste moon lingers - hangs in the air, parallel, kissing the tree canopy with the watery sun, in ascendant. It looks like an eclipse could happen, a sky obliterating Armageddon that would be the answer to Elsbeth's prayer, to be out of this place, off this earth. Elsbeth's light is dimming, the foetus erasing her life-force, junk, addiction, and a bloated stomach spittling the candle's flame. The world had revolved around Elsie, Beth, Els, Elsbo, Becks, Becky, Bex, and now she is the bit part-player, no longer the fulcrum, and she is not prepared.

The radiator below the window comes on, she can feel the warmth rising, but she remains cold. She moves to the bed, opens the bag, and changes into togs that nearly harmonise. Sloppy jeans that sit below her tummy, a ripped white t-shirt, and grey sweat top, faded Russell logo stamped across the chest, the closest she'll ever get to sport. Incongruous, but great on her, the shabby worn in look accentuates her unprocessed allure, hair tipping over the mottled grey. She pulls on socks and boots. In the bathroom are three fresh towels on a rack above the radiator, the tiling and porcelain shining with freshness and lack of use. She goes to toilet, checks her face, washes her hands, and uses water cupped in them to swallow a handful of pills. The window reveals below a new deep-green Land Rover parked out front, the aluminium treadboard box-top on the rear indicating someone of country tendencies. "Oh, not the doctor," already knowing her mother's game. Eileen's Imp is there, but father's Jaguar is gone, the indentation in the limestone chippings showing where it had been. "Here we go," Elsbeth plods to face the music, the mild buzz from indeterminate medication starting to numb the unpleasant withdrawal side-effects, it was now twenty four hours since she'd properly jacked-up.

Dogs go crazy, two bundling big Labradors, golden, friendly, shimmy on the shiny red quarry tiles, nails clattering, barking at Elsbeth's entry. "Lovelies!!" Elsbeth kneels and greets them like they're hers, ruffling each muzzle. They chase between their owner, and Elsbeth, as if there is a fast conveyer belt transporting them between the table and door.

"AMANDA!" Elsbeth immediately pegs the interloper, sat at the table with Eileen, the same positions she and Michaela had taken the last time she'd used the kitchen.

"Christ, darling, look at you!" Amanda rising, the epitome of prosperity, she runs, clutches her old school-pal, they part, Amanda pushing her back, holding her static whilst she surveys the whole of Elsbeth, " darling, you look amazing! How long is it? I couldn't believe it when your Mum said!" The dogs are jumping, scratching at clothing, over-excited, jammy saliva deposited everywhere, over feet and floor.

"SPANNER, WRENCH, DOWN!" They mooch, calming. "David named them not me!" Amanda excusing the pretentious monikers. "Hello?!" Elsbeth answers, the past starting to recompile. "Come over, you must come over, tonight, there's so much to talk about darling!" Eileen, in dressing-gown and slippers, is ready for Elsbeth, "Tea, coffee, there's toast, cereal, juice, I can do eggs, what would you like darling, you had a good sleep?" Eileen lifts up off the stool, ready to fuss. Amanda takes Elsbeth's hand authoritatively, almost skipping back to the table, like she'd found the bone she's been looking for. She sits Elsbeth next to her. Amanda is radiant in a ruddy way, stout red cheeks, once endearing and sweet, are now plain chubby, she's put on weight. She fills her jeans with wide thighs, and a man's peregrine natural wool jumper, with four inch zipper, covers her ample frame. The dogs circle Amanda's Wellingtons, and eventually lie against the seat legs occasionally nuzzling each other. "Not sure if I'm ready. I wasn't expecting this, Mummy?" Eileen answers, half-embarrassed, she's facing the other way, putting toast in, "We kept in touch, Amanda's done well in business, haven't you Amanda? And she has a job for you." Amanda, now uncomfortable, reaches for the large coffee mug, takes a bite of toast, and talks with her mouth full, "Well, only when you want, there is an…" Elsbeth places her hand on Amanda's arm, sweetly, "That's brilliant, thank you Amanda, I'll get this un-loaded first," and she pats her lump. Amanda laughs and the friction clears. "I've got three, I could never lose weight, look at me, you're so skinny, I'm very jealous darling," Amanda slaps her rump, "I porked up and it never left." The toaster pops, and Eileen places the slices in front of Elsbeth, butters it, hoping she will eat. Elsbeth finally

Elsbeth disconsolately placing her hands in her jean pockets and leaning back against the Jeep, as if William will have to answer to her. He has his head lowered and parks far enough from the Land Rover so as not to engage, but Amanda has other ideas. She does a mini-wave with both hands as if mimicking a butterfly taking off. He is forced to wave, and half-smile. William gets out, he has untidy ill-fitting jeans on, black office brogues requisitioned for gardening, and a brown padded anorak, zipped to the neck, threadbare cotton checked shirt collars sprouting from the top. He shouts, "I'm going to get the barrow!" "Want a hand?!" Amanda returns, with Elsbeth chiming in-between, "Hi Daddy, I'll get it!" He's already scrammed, racing, on the side path by the house. The mossy sandstone flags are slippery from the rain, and he nearly trips, "That's okay, I got it!"

"You don't know half, darling," Amanda addresses Elsbeth, "I'll tell you later, he's not himself anymore." They hug, and Elsbeth sees Amanda off. The drive is empty, Elsbeth pivots surveying the huge plot, isolated in the greyness, nods her head and mumbles, "Christ, what am I doing here." She crunches her way to the Jag, and clicks the boot open. There are three bags of compost, and a new rake sitting on an old check blanket. She sits on the edge and waits to help her father, but he doesn't come, so she gives up and goes in, shutting the boot.

Eileen is dressed, and cooking lunch in the kitchen, seems breezy, obviously buoyed by Amanda's support. There is only just a snatch of time to fill before eating, and Elsbeth is subjected to another Beckett style snub from her father, over-compensated for in bales by her mother. The afternoon is equally as packed, and routine conventionality is suppressing Elsbeth's nervous system yearning. At the private surgery, in Woking, Elsbeth won't see the doctor with her mother, and there is a minor row, her Mum surrendering, and waiting an hour reading magazines. Dr. Richard doesn't seem to have aged to Elsbeth, then perhaps he was always oldish, and a few more years hasn't made any difference. His office is as she remembers, spacious, wholesome, practical, dominated by a significant oak desk. Dr. Richard is handsome in a 1970's sitcom kindly university professor mode, trim beard, and spotless white coat. Money counts, and Elsbeth gets what she needs, barbiturates, and morphine in truck-loads. She has changed her mind about the visit, her mother was right. He does an examination, gets the nurse to take blood for further tests, but she refuses a hospital visit for a scan. She 'doesn't trust it, it'll harm the baby'. He is sympathetic, he's heard every type of neuroses, his moneyed clients include rock stars and actors who've tested his medical agility over the years. She can smell his aftershave, it's musky, yet hygienic, as he examines the track marks on her willowy arms. He has a silvery re-assuring tone, "They've taken a fair lot of abuse, I suggest you don't use this anymore." Elsbeth is frank, "I use my foot." She feels comfortable with him, as she did as a little girl.

"Don't inject anymore, for the baby's sake. The morphine dose is very strict, pills, it can have detrimental effects, it's just heroin anyway, without the rubbish in it, and the barbiturates are to take the edge off. The idea is, we are decreasing, it'll take time, you've got to persevere, I'm making an appointment with the specialist, privately, and I need you here next week for the next prescription. It's very important, and flush the heroin, you'll kill your baby."
Elsbeth nods, sheepish.

"Don't worry, I've seen it all, and we want you and the baby better, don't we?"

"Yes doctor."

He writes, it's quiet, she stares, it's Latin, she can't make out the scrawl.

"What happened to Daddy?"

"Hasn't your mother told you?"

"No, I can't…."

"It's no ordinary prescription, it'll be delivered, before six, I'll give the pharmacy a call, you can't just get this from Timothy Whites," he laughs at his own joke, rips off the slip, goes to her side of the desk, and hands it to her, "give this to Maureen at reception, who'll do next weeks' time as well," handing it to her, "it's fantastic to have you back," he takes her hand, "I was there at your birth… we all love you."

Elsbeth crumples and starts to cry.

"I'll get Eileen."

"No, no," she grabs a tissue out of the box on the desk, I'm alright, thank you doctor Richard." She stands, drying her eyes, gives him a hug and leaves.

Elsbeth and Eileen could be any wealthy mother and

daughter out on a shopping spree in town, except Elsbeth blacks out, stone-cold, asleep, during tea and cake in Harvey's top-floor restaurant, dribbling on the table, her head knocking liquid everywhere. Eileen is flustered, and a waiter helps, waking Elsbeth and mopping up.

At home, Elsbeth gets ready to see Amanda and her clan. William is watching the news in his den when Elsbeth knocks and enters. He doesn't look up. It's dark, one low level floor lamp. Eileen told her not to go in, it used to be his office, but she's ignored her. She's been killing time in the hall and living room waiting for the pharmaceuticals promised by the doctor, wanting a hit before she goes out. Elsbeth is a bit desperate and nervy, having exhausted heroin in her bag, and it only containing various uppers and pain-killers. She has her hippy look, but it's revised, with items bought by her mother in the afternoon, giving a sophisticated edge, a skirt short but pleated with large Scottish checks, dark wool tights, boots, big belt, and spangley halter-neck top, layers for the cold, and a thick woollen king knit scarf. Her hair is up, piled on her head, held by claws, which is unusual and it highlights her sleek neck. One wouldn't distinguish her as being pregnant. "Hi Daddy, what's on?" She approaches, standing behind his chair, the programme uninterrupted. He doesn't move, or acknowledge her, then, "Strikes, strikes, strikes." He sounds a trifle annoyed, then clams up, the newscaster bleats on.

Elsbeth views the room, there are still the bookcases, lined with financial, management reference books, used in William's profession, but more, lots of gardening books and magazines, the desk gone. The high windows have the best aspect of the grounds, and the curtains haven't been shut, despite the darkness. The moon visible, a sprinkling of stars, it cleared up in the afternoon, the miniscule appearance of sun scuppered by a 4 pm sunset. There is the globe drinks cabinet, it looks unused, William no longer needing it after his breakdown. The side table next to his chair has a half drunk cup of tea, plate of biscuits, crumbs where a couple have been eaten, and a gardening catalogue open at the seeds pages in the back, a couple of summer packs ringed with blue pen, the biro sitting on the open page. The tiny print mail-order form is completed at the bottom, ready to be cut-out and posted with a cheque. The chair is deep supple leather, mended in places, and covered with a large rug. He has his feet up, be-socked, on a matching leather pouf, it too has seen better days. Elsbeth clutches the head of the chair, not knowing what to do with herself now. There is an atmosphere, and she's wishing she hadn't come in, "Your desk used to be there." He has a TV lazybones remote, connected to the television by a long wire, and he turns the volume up loud. Elsbeth talks over, "I'm going out, to see Amanda, I won't be having supper tonight, have a nice evening." She pats him on the shoulders like a nurse might comfort a patient, and gets going, shutting the door behind, but is helped by her Mother, who has just come from the kitchen. Eileen is rankled, and takes the handle, covering Elsbeth's hand, to ensure it clicks shut.

"He can't be disturbed," she whispers.

"Why Mummy, what happened?" Elsbeth somewhat defensive.

"Kevin is here to get you, he came round the back."

"Why don't you tell me mother?"

"Now isn't the time, that's his space."

"Cool, I've got to wait for my prescription," Elsbeth's anger quickly disperses, as ever, "I'll come and talk to Kevin."

They both continue in the direction of the kitchen.

"Oh, they came ages ago," Eileen remembering, "when you were in the bath, it's the delivery service, brings your Dad's as well."

"What's he on then?"

"He's not *on* anything," her mother's disgruntled, "they're just his heart pills, blood pressure, you know."

Eileen stops, retracing, as if forgetting, then knocks on the den door again, and disappears inside.

The packs of pills sit next to Kevin who's propped against the Aga, drinking tea and gorging the same biscuits that William had, custard creams and digestives. "You'll get fat on those," Elsbeth chirps. Kevin sports a Groundsman Willie beard, shapeless oatmeal overalls and clodhopper boots. He's of indeterminate age, facial hair hiding the wrinkling process that commenced many years prior.

"Cheeky bitch," he has west country accent that seems put-on, as he's lived in Surrey for forty years.

"I know you, you used to do the lawns at The Pines, you worked with your Dad, always wolf-whistling us, dirty git," Elsbeth throws cheek back his way.

"Kev to you," he laughs, "that's a long while ago, surprised you remember that, your luck coulda been in."

"It would be in now if you weren't such a hairy fat cobbler."

"Ha, ha, you got me there, Miss Mandy warned me about you!"

"Yeah, I hope it's all bad, let's go Kev."

Eileen re-enters and makes a beeline for Elsbeth pressing thirty pounds into her hand, trying to hide it from Kevin, "Get a cab home darling, Amanda's got the number, we'll be in bed." Kevin sees what's happening, "Don't worry Miss Eileen, I'm bringing 'er back, Miss Mandy's given instructions." Eileen pushes it into Elsbeth's fluffed Kaftan pocket as the recipient palm is defiant, "Send my love to Amanda." Eileen gives her last goodbye, then calls again when they're at the back door,

"It's golf after breakfast Elsbeth, don't forget! And, the key is in the usual place!" "Cool, okay Mummy, bye."

"Alright Miss Eileen, thank you," Kevin pipes.

They trail round the house, the outside lights are on, they get to the Range Rover and Elsbeth hikes in, he shuts her door, she's showing some leg, and Kevin's heart races. Elsbeth has the chemist

bag, roots in, pops a couple of morphine without looking at the label,

or dosage, reaches for the gum in her pocket, pushing the money

deeper, and offers Kevin a slip before unwrapping a slice herself.

She sits and chews, opens the window part-way, and turns the radio

on, skipping through the channels. Kevin half watches her side on,

he is concentrating on the lanes, the darkness making them difficult

to navigate.

"You live in the middle of nowhere, you do."

"I don't live here," she answers smoothly whilst finding a pirate

station, Caroline buzzes in, an American psych band.

"You look like you live somewhere right trendy, all beyond me I'm

afraid." Elsbeth ignores him, raises her boots up on the dash, her

skirt edging back further, her sweet beauty is now imbibed with

divine self-assuredness, a swaggering belligerence part confidence,

part drugs. She hums to the track, and Kevin shuts up. The

driveway up to Bentley Hill is enough to put off anyone living there,

just for the drawn-out pain of getting to the front door, it criss-

crosses a brook, two bridges, the house looming bigger and bigger,

solid red-brick, three massive floors, and it's lit up like Christmas, cars everywhere. Before getting out she pops another morphine, a natural sense of how much is needed by the buzz she received from the previous two.

"What's all that Miss Elsbeth?"

"Oh, just for the pregnancy, for morning sickness."

He goes to the other side to sort out her door.

"You're pregnant?!"

"Un-huh."

Kevin patronisingly gives her a little instruction, "Go up and ring the bell, Miss Mandy's there, when you need me, I'll be in the kitchen, I'll drop you back home."

"Thanks Kevin!" she is ebullient, giving him a huge kiss, he's knocked out, and she bounces off. Elsbeth is fabulous, and feels sixteen. The drugs are left in the door-well, and he rifles when she is out of sight.

Amanda does answer the door, and the hall is rammed, people, children, dogs, a racket, Rod Stewart's 'Maggie May' playing over super-big Bang & Olufsen speakers, they tower in the corners like chrome and veneer flying saucers. Amanda is on the verge of apoplexy that Elsbeth is here, virtually speechless, a long

embrace disables Elsbeth, who manages, "Hi darling." She looks up

and around over Amanda's shoulder, as she won't release. The

reception resembles a Jacobean court, the upper floors are balconies,

looking directly onto them, like The Globe, but ultra-modern and

cheerful. The floor has chess-board, black and white tiles, and the

stair-case rises like an optical illusion, as it laps over itself. "This

place is remarkable Amanda, how much money have you got!"

Amanda finally eases up, still holding Elsbeth close, a grip on both

arms, "It was Daddy's, don't you remember? We had the whole

place done, everything ripped out, virtually re-built it!" Elsbeth

sways her head, "No, I just don't remember." It's as if they're on a

waltzing amusement ride. "Want a drink darling, a lemonade or... I

know you can't drink....?" Elsbeth replies, "Oh no, I'll have wine,

white wine, I won't have much." "Right!" Amanda announcing and

releasing Elsbeth, she marches through the legions, Elsbeth follows.

There is a parting of the way for them, Elsbeth 'viewed'. Elsbeth

can see her shape properly now. Amanda's wearing an

uncomplimentary front-slit sky-blue dress, and cream-silk court

shoes. It owes more to Beverley Moss than Jerry Hall, and her thick dull brown hair, more suited to the Scottish winters her ancestors endured, than the Surrey rolling valleys, welded into a flick-under that would underscore a highland fling for The Royal Scots Dragoon bagpipes. Motherhood and life has manhandled her features into pieces of chunky play-dough. Elsbeth cruelly thinks, 'no wonder she needs a friend'. Wine is delivered, children and husband paraded. He, David, is six foot tall, not the expected matching for Amanda, quite trendy and very sociable, hits it off with Elsbeth, he's in advertising, and has a great interest in the arts. Elsbeth reels off her favourites with flourishes, wine slopping in one hand, an imaginary maraca attractively shaking in the other as she gesticulates. David has a little goatee, sloppy bohemian jumper, black jeans. He met Amanda at Cambridge, both on fine arts, and Amanda 'chucked it in', when her Dad passed, called to run the business. "Shame," he shouts over the noise, "she would have made a great writer… or journalist!" Virtually her whole company is there, management, partners, relatives, her Mum, who Elsbeth endures for a good twenty minutes. She escapes to the toilet and plugs a morphine, bending over, siding her knickers in the cubicle. She can hear Amanda shouting, Elsbeth checks her look, her eyes are pasted, she feels good, twiddles with her hair inconsequentially, and the door handle turns, someone is next. She opens it to a mini-Amanda. "Everyone is going out for the Fireworks!" the ten year old excitedly exclaims. "Cool," comes the answer, and Elsbeth tags along. Coats are being retrieved, drinks grabbed, the hall is emptying, Amanda directing. David sees Elsbeth, "You come with me and the kids!" Elsbeth mouths and points to the bottles, "Just get another drink."

He waits alone for her, 'Tumbling Dice' comes on the stereo, and Elsbeth dances. A rocket ship has landed and aliens from the planet Wonder have taken over the earth. He nearly cries with joy watching her, he's invisible. Elsbeth's on celestial cloud Elsbeth, and could easily be Mick or Keith's squeeze. It finishes, The Osmonds' 'Down By The Lazy River' takes over. Elsbeth laughs uncontrollably, running her hands so they stroke her legs, bending slightly.
"Sorry!"
David is embarrassed, "No, let me!" He gets the drink, a new glass of wine. They traipse through the kitchens, they're like a hotel's, stainless steel, and extraction units. "Amanda designed all this, we

entertain a lot!"

"Cool."

Out back, there's a stone patio the size of Heathrow runway three, two chefs roasting a hog, barbecues, tables laid with bread rolls for hotdogs, twinkly lights. Elsbeth sups it up, "Oh, Jesus, this is something." David smiles, "Amanda never does anything by halves." The three kids, including Amanda junior run about with the other children, the lawns are lit up with green and red floodlights, fireworks launch on the other side of the lake, there are cheers, and each battery glimmers in misty Autumn waters. Amanda is with her parents. "Where do they live now then?" Elsbeth indicates, David, with relief, "We got a Bungalow for them, this place needs kids and people!"

"Oh!" There's a huge bang that takes Elsbeth off guard, and a multi-rocket shoots up splintering into blue and red arrows burning out in the fog over the lake. "It's amazing," she laughs, straightening out her leg, and rotating her foot, finishing her drink in one.

"I'll show you around, I've got a Gilbert & George drawing, c'mon!"

"Cool."

They're right by the double-doors, go back through the kitchens, Elsbeth grabbing more wine from the bottles lined up there, and David directs them via the stairs once reserved for staff. He gives a running commentary, music is echoing by itself, T.Rex, and explosions thud outside. They have a view over the activities below, the fireworks are thumping, ooh's and aah's seeping in via the window. David has artwork everywhere and his interests, it's a cornucopia of modern art, guitars, records, a big system, record deck, tape machines, massive KEF speakers, bare floors, rugs, television and armchairs. The room is warehouse-like, the art illuminated with half a dozen downlighters.

"This is my little cubbyhole, the kids aren't allowed, you know what I mean."

"Hmm, not really, it's not exactly small."

Elsbeth flits around fingering, examining the hangings attentively, David explains them as if he picked them up in the village hall jumble sale, rather than the actual truth, from major exhibitions, and dealer networks. They reach the Gilbert & George, massive tree lined pencil scribblings, with the gay lovers centre stage. "Hmm, it's a little plain," Elsbeth opines. "Really?" David's disappointed.

Elsbeth slugs more of the wine. "I know something that'll open your mind to it," David fixes directly at her. "Oh yeh?" Elsbeth has heard it all before, she's been offered every narcotic inducement over the years, "what then?" David pulls a medicine bottle from his pocket, "I know a friendly dentist," takes her hand, turns it, and strips a line of the cocaine along her wrist. It sits there, her hand immobile as he repeats the action on his own and sniffs the line. He snorts hard, wipes the excess and eats it, "Go on then." She follows suit and her hair falls free slightly, one of the clasps coming loose, so she shakes it out as she rolls her head backwards, "Fuck!" He leans in and snogs her, tongues caress, and she pushes herself into him, he takes her, what little skin covers her sides he grabs, they fall to the rug, he pulls her tights and pants off, she undoes his jeans, tugging them to his knees, and he digs a hole in his marriage. Mid-spade they take more cocaine. Amanda opens the door, they hadn't noticed the show outside had halted, and David wasn't at his post. David attempts to speak, she marches out, and Elsbeth takes possession of the cocaine bottle from his pocket as he fumbles with his pants, trying to pull them back up. Elsbeth, nonvocal, just sits on her bum, as soon as he gets off, and puts her underwear back on. "Sorry, Christ," he is panicking.

"It's fine, you didn't come… did you?"

He is flustered, "Wow, you're something else."

He is out of the room. She steals the Gilbert & George, rolling it under her coat, and walks off, leaving the house. With the shouting, and huge set-to in the gleaming kitchens nobody notices her slipping out front, with a bottle of white. She goes to the Range Rover to get her pharmaceuticals but Kevin is there, smoking. He has been there for a bit, so he's ignorant of the unravelling at Amanda-central.

"You ready for your lift home Miss Elsbeth?"

"Yes, okay, thank you Kevin, that's very sweet."

"Would you like a cigarette Miss Elsbeth?"

"No, that's okay, it's bad for the baby."

Eileen is at the front door, William behind her. She is glaring, him sheepish, the reception lights are on, as well as the outside lamps. They're in their dressing gowns and slippers. Distant wallops saturate the air, bonfire night armaments pant across Surrey, burns, "None of us have ever, seen, eerrr, experienced anything like it, we need a prognosis, I can't just start messing around in there, there are solutions, but… we need X-Rays, nurse?" "Like I was saying doctor, that's the problem, there's a danger in moving him, all that's keeping him alive is that thing, Colin is weak, the mother is a heroin addict, and the wee one is suffering… it's terrible." She starts to weep, bags are showing under her eyes, she has a greying perm, now a mop with stress and 'running-ragged', "I've never… never seen, poor little fellow, what.. what can we do? The nurses… they won't go in there, there's only two who can… who are willing." "Okay, okay," Davis gives her a tissue, and puts his hand on her back, being the closest, "let's make decisions, we've got to follow a plan, we need to start." Felixson begins, he's fatigued, "Look we can only do what's within our realms of experience, there's obviously growth, Paget's disease perhaps, but on the exterior? Major deformities, Elephantiasis, Proteus Syndrome, whatever, genetic disorder. Let's line up tests for the parents, unearth, genealogy, family history…" Davis interrupts, "I have some knowledge of the family, well not…" Felixson continues over him, "…so on, and in the meantime keep him going for a couple of days, take blood samples, and get X-Rays, whatever the outcome, get drips in there, treat the Neonatal Abstinence Syndrome, keep Colin on methadone, reduce the dose daily, can you write a prescription please Dr. Savage?"

"Yeah, sure, I'll see to it, and the feeds." Davis is as assured as his studious bespectacled glare, "I'll liaise with him upstairs, Sir Edmund, when he's back on Monday, let's meet, how about, two nights, Monday evening, 7 pm, can you get the X-Rays here for then nurse?" Nurse Spain chokes, "If I can find people who will do it." Felixson, " I will do it if necessary, it's a bloody hospital, I can work a radiology machine, it's not rocket science." Davis, "Right doctor, it'll get organised, let me liaise with the union, we can't cover you for that." Felixson takes a turned up cheese sandwich, "I need a drink I've been in here since 6 am." They rise, picking up their papers, stubbing out cigarettes, and make to go. "Oh, what about the mother?" Savage refers to his clipboard, "Elsbeth, Elsbeth Henderson?" Davis turns back, "I was trying to say, kid gloves, she's daughter of business magnate Willy Henderson, made a killing in stocks, I know their consultant, Richard Hartley, he's my neighbour. Bloody mess, pater went off his rocker, his wife was having an affair with a surgeon, remember Stanley, struck off. Old man had a breakdown and a double coronary, Elsbeth did a runner, tragedy, they couldn't get her back, ended up with this loser…" Savage, "Well at least we know they're good English stock, let's pull apart the father's side, see if there's any background, in-breeding, he sounds like a dago." Katsura, "Fuckin' christ, what year is this, 1947? Why not round them all up and gas them." Felixson, "Bloody good idea Kats, first one tonight… at least I'd get one bloody good night's sleep."

Django and Gash are in the corridor, a bench of unrelenting plastic chairs keep their bums company, whilst they wait the eternal wait. The walls are pink below a thick brown-stained wooden dado rail, that which stops moving iron beds taking a chunk out of the plaster, and above that, NHS brown, whitewashed ceilings, and unforgiving strip lights. There are moth-eared posters, 'Use Medicines Properly', and 'Don't Smuggle Death' warning of rabies posted, with a timetable for visiting hours along the passage. Police stand at the far end, outside the door of Colin, and Elsbeth is across the way, opposite in her own room. The police don't know if there are any charges, but the two officers are instructed to keep Django out, he can only sit at the end of the fish-eye lens, patiently interviewing the doctors and nurses who've been rushing by for the past twelve hours, runny concrete, mostly platitudes. The previous night has turned into another. Everyone is still alive, but they've lost touch with the outside world, and any sense of reality, or the type of reality that Django hitherto subscribed to. Gash removes his hat, and un-gaffas packets of speed. Django who's head is in his hands, eyes closed, senses Gash's actions, and slams the hat across the hall. The speed goes flying, pills everywhere, the police glare. Gash goes on all fours and starts retrieving the dexys.

"You better go Gash," Django never calls him by his name. Gash realises his misdemeanor, "No, I'll stay, I'm going to the café to get some food and water Djang'," he rises, scooping up his cap, back into place. The pills remain. Tasleen and Johnno went home a couple of hours after the incident, Johnno had gone straight to work, taking a palm's-worth of Gash's pep-pills, he'd been up for two days, he still had to tackle a double-shift at Tottenham garage. He'd sleep the lunch hour, and any breaks. He couldn't lose his job. Gash walks off, his Cubans click on the vinyl floor tiles, Django looks up, directions, and Elsbeth wouldn't be discharged until she's completely well, which could be weeks or months. Django can feel he's being hoodwinked, "This can't be right," he repeats, for the benefit of the administrator, and himself.

Django's on his own now. Thinking straight hasn't been his forte for many years. A fog is lifting, and he doesn't mind it. He intends to head back to Notting Hill, to walk, he has no money. Django stumbles over steps, working his way through the warren of wards, comings-and-goings, other people's travails notched in their features. He sees black hole eyes, tearful middle-aged parents, sickly children, porters transporting the infirm in beds that look like they should be static, heavy mechanised contraptions unique to terminal institutions. It has a profound effect. It makes him feel young, a little refreshed, reassured, pleased to be alive, happy that Elsbeth and Colin are alive, convincing himself he saved his son, "That wouldn't have happened in a hospital," he says to himself. Django is a butterfly emerging from a cocoon he's been wrapped in for thirteen years.

The St. Thomas's exit is the via the Doric colonnade, and the grandness of the Tuscan columns buoy Django, reminding of his hometown, and he almost has a spring in his step; he has persevered, he's a father, Elsbeth's alright.

Out on to the busy Lambeth Palace Road Django's accosted, two guys, one with a camera, the other a portable tape recorder. They have a similar demeanour, and are being caught up by three more, which've come running from the far entrance, at Guy's. The first one stops Django walking by standing in front of him, he's small, smaller than Django anyway, forties, a bit twisted, like he has arthritis, his leg extends, foot bent upwards at thirty degrees to the ground, mimicking a bike stand. He's obviously a pro at the stopping move, and Django's a bit lost as to where to advance, the rest rallying in a pincer movement. Pedestrians part, and stare. Django checks for escape routes, not thoroughly computing, but it doesn't take long. A few flashes go, they've got a close up of Daddy ConeBoy.

"Hang on, hang on, please, Mr. Biancho?" the arthritic one bids. He thrusts the microphone, and thumps the tape into record, "How's

A recovering junky, and recovering patient, they'd bustled inside her ovaries, ensured she was unable have any more kids (god forbid!), repaired the home birthing fiasco, and then the pressure from her parents, Django, Dr. Richard, et al. The entire caboodle was cushioned by Henderson privilege.

Django irradiates the street, eventually arriving mid-afternoon. He hitched a couple of lifts, an odd activity in London, but a van driver gets him as far as Hyde Park, then an air-hostess on her way to Heathrow out via Bayswater Road. She didn't want to let him go, despite his ragged appearance and stink, but he jumps out in traffic between Lancaster Gate and Notting Hill striding up back streets to the familial. Parishioners smile at his bouncing into The Grove, like he hadn't been gone, as if bugger-all had happened. His swarthy Roman charm broke any hardened nut, he is the establishment in these parts. He's offered the usual packets on the way in, "Thanks man, not now." Music blasts from windows, Steel Pulse and Wire, echo in a dubby punk-reggae mash-up, beats an overlapping hash. Django is so accustomed to the haunt he doesn't notice the house is shuttered like a prison. No.10 has an iron security door, and windows. They are the style that is impossible to prise open, with a massive solid bar protruding from a letter-box affair that connects to a bar at right angles on the inside, which spans the whole frame. One can't get to the frame to remove it, as the steel-plate outside covers it. An impregnable Ingersol padlock, the type councils employ to board up their repossessions secures the complete system. Upstairs windows have sheet-metal nailed across them. A sign is taped to the front door, it's laminated, CLOSED, without reading it entirely he gets the gist, doesn't want to venture closer, burying the meaning, like he's buried other responsibility throughout his life. An optician's sight test chart, text size decreases as it descends, the most important stuff mini-print, like terms and conditions on a hire purchase agreement contrived to leave one in debt, forever. 'Condemned' and 'Royal Borough of Kensington and Chelsea', pulse in his cranium. Django stands at the gate, an arm each side, voiles of anger and heartbreak rejoinder in the pit of his stomach, a causality in his bowel. A curdle, he's hungry but not. He curves up between the broken up brick pillars, his back against one, feet pressing the other, head in hands. No money, homeless, but he's had it good for a bit, longer than most people. Twelve years, one

Kate is a wave rider, a chaser, a hitter, morphing into fashion guru, using ConeBoy money to start a band, lead a band, create a brand. Soaking up copious pitfalls from the wastrel punk outfits she'd hung around, she easily learns to pump out the four chords required for dumb A&R men to lasciviously lap up her trajectory of Sigue Sigue Sputnik new-wave. A couple of punky shampoo'ey hits and a massive Japanese following allow Kate to carve a merchandising corner, fashion range, concessions, and to clean up. Twenty years would see her swanning in her swanky New York offices, taking calls from Madonna and Kate Blanchet.

Django and Kate face each-other, fish out of water at the small table, and dimly lit micro-kitchen. A window faces back gardens and yards, pitch black out, below which is a stainless steel sink, any remains of stainless erased by bleach, and scrubbing brushes, then a draining board, and cupboards. The door opposite leads directly to a living space that fronts the house, and faces No.10. Off this, Johnno's box bedroom. It's near enough proper accommodation, bar the toilet and bath on the upstairs landing, shared with four other tenants. It's damp, dark and dingy, but splattered with colourful Caribbean throws, paintings, indigenous art, and Tasleen's vibrant paint splashings. She has done her best.

Django and Kate, the odd couple, they've known each other, but don't know each other one bit. Django had held court at No.10, people moved in and out, a Warholian Factory minus the productiveness, but proceedings were under a haze, they'd ducked, glassy, flirted with narcotics, people throwing the dice to a Luke Rhinehart soundtrack.

Here, in the moment, wide eyed. Django can see the black in the centre of Kate's pupil, and she the crystal in his, like a dart from the Aegean. Their souls bare, Django sober, Kate moneyed up, there is serenity in the old kitchen that's been meticulously fancied up by Tasleen's dexterity. Conversation's minimalist, Django knows what's required, and Kate doesn't need to do much to assuage him. She is an agent, on the gravy train. He poignantly comprehends his situation; adrift, penniless, excluded from hospital consultations, he is powerless. No clout, insignificant, he doesn't matter, the pendulum has swung to The Henderson's. They have the providence to re-claim their daughter, and possess their Grandson whatever the child's disability. Eileen and William host a Ferry Terminal of love to bursting, that which drained from their relationship and needed unleashing elsewhere. It can pour like over-sweetened Clotted Cream turned with Brandy Butter coating an oversized Victorian cartoon-bomb shape Christmas pudding, lit up with a tumbler of cooking brandy. Django is relegated, not even second class, he's the minority, and Kate is proposing a quick fix. He is up against a wall, the victim. Django slides the card from his jeans pocket on to the table.

MAX DACRE

REPORTER

DAILY MIRROR

01-780 3209

She passes the envelope, he goes to bed and she leaves. He is the melting cheese to her fondue burner, she the tiered tower to his chocolate fountain. They could fancy each other, but the sense of disaster, bereavement and oddness, renders those feelings inappropriate. This is a business arrangement.

The light streams in, clattering on the street wakes Django, there is no-one home. He has breakfast, cereal Tasleen has left next to a spare key, and up in the bathroom, he has a fast bath, washes his hair, cleans his teeth and puts clean clothes on. He empties Elsbeth's bag, finds the drawing, squared up, and flattens it out on the living-room floor, leaving it there.

Django is at the Labour Exchange by ten, but there are already two queues out of the door of the stained brick offices at Kensal Road. Four tellers sit at barred windows, the far end of the room, then another, un-manned to the far left, with a sign up, 'personal issue - wait to be called'. There are two steps up to the apertures, so each applicant must fawn, as if asking to approach a Judge at the bar. A kind of intimidation that also relieves the clerks of a good deal of abuse, since signees are cut down to size before they even get to the designated port hole. It's about waiting, patiently, and it gives time for Django to think. That's been impossible, such is the propulsion of events of the past two days. The lines plough achingly slow, and Django's ossifying, as, even though he's not signed on before, or had a proper job, he has brown cards with expert precision relentlessly, sometimes referring a punter to an interview, where they'll be presented with a range of useless jobs to traipse after, because they've been unemployed for two years or more. The majority go nowhere, due to the number of applicants, but the process must be adhered to. Others are referred to the personal issue window, where they hang around for cash.

Mainly it's the bashing of the signing-on card day-after-day with an inked, dated, adjustable-stamp, and futile questioning, delivered in a dank monotone.

'Have you been looking for work in the past two weeks?'…….

'Have you had any work in the past two weeks?'

Answer 'Yes' and your money is stopped, fresh applications are required, and it can take up to eleven weeks to get another payment cheque. Also, you're holding up the queue behind you. Two meandering rows are stupid as well, and, the occasional plucky patron will bravely undertake to unify the pair, with tricky military barbing, fruitlessly. There's no logical explanation, only a plethora of psychological theories, since men aren't in one and women in another, or, young in one, and old in the other. Outside, the pavement has two directions, left and right, so people approach from both. It's churlish to disallow someone approaching from the left the option to join at the left, even if there's already a queue started on the right. Thus people join both ends, generally stay-put, committed to their column, regardless of impetus. Django's chosen well, moving forward at a reasonable rate, and finds solace in the stir-fry of claimants. Thirty minutes to an hour is the usual scale, and he is near the kiosks. Far from being a free-for-all when heading up the queue, the system takes hold, and finger comely wagging allows the window-women to choose their patients at the front. It disperses the front-runners rapidly, there's little purpose in jostling, and, it's at this juncture one must carefully survey the three available windows for your signage. All-in-all this system has the desired effect, each participant is grateful for being a chosen-one, especially picked out.

The British penchant for reticence has hardly imbued Django and the divide-and-rule technique is lost on him. He takes the two steps up, without prejudice, expectation, or fear. The young girl looks up from the list, and the bars and glass in front of her evaporate, as she surveys what she hopes could be her date for the evening. Django melodiously explains in his deep Italian tinged tone, whilst she thinks he's smouldering. Pale, with a piked face, slender neck, couple of necklaces, she has a dusky yellow blouse on, with small rounded collars which concentrates her watery complexion, then, a slight ruffle, that disappears below a navy woollen tabard dress of zero shape. She is glued to his predicament, already rehearsed in his head, he gives Johnno's address, and she serves him personal issue, another signing on date for two weeks hence, and a personal adviser appointment which he never attends. She stares at his address, hoping her flirtyness will make him connect it to her. He's oblivious, other things on his mind. As he descends the steps, her gaze follows, and she hesitates a little too long before making the miserable come-hither finger at the next candidate. In half an hour Django has seen the cash-commissar, and rammed the five ten pound notes in his jeans pocket, by the cheque. Mugging does happen, but not today. He heads to the bank on the corner, opposite, and opens an account with the cheque, again giving Johnno's address. They don't ask for identification, fraud is expected, or hoped for. He pays an additional £10 to fast track it, goes into the post-office two doors on, buys a notepad and pens. In the Wimpy Django writes a to-do list, in Italian, over tea and toast, and watches the extending wait'ees, outside the greying Victorian plug-hole. He hasn't properly learned to write in English. Returning to the bank, he's kept waiting, then withdraws £900 leaving £100 in the account. He gets a bus to Oxford Street, buys a cheap off the shelf dark suit in Moss Bros, then back to Johnno's, where he leaves £500 in an envelope on the kitchen table for Tasleen. He eats a sandwich made from bits Tasleen has in her tiny fridge and stares out of the living room window at his house, boarded up. It's difficult to recall one day or night spent there, and he only feels an unquenchable yearning that's bigger than him, to have the ones he loves close, to replicate the sonorousness of unity, the serenity of coupling. No. 10 is dead. He packs Elsbeth's school case with clothes that he thinks she'll want, and walks to the tube station at Ladbroke Grove, where he calls his landlord from the phonebox, in an effort to get an explanation. The other end clicks off when Django speaks, he tries again, and it clicks off, and now Django knows where he stands. He's been collecting rents for this guy for ten years, since he's been on The Grove. "Bastardo," he mumbles.

At the hospital Django tries visiting his son and partner. The prestigious 'classic' hue. They are popular again, and have been forced to reform. By the time they get on stage together, they'll be uniformly styled, as a working unit, but satisfactorily diverse to allow their characters to blossom, and to wallow in their own genius. Mature and with iconic status, but by the end of the tour they'll be travelling with their own entourages in separate buses, staying in different hotels, ego disabling any prospect of banking the millions quaffed in absurd petulant tour expenses. Django would leave ten shows before the end of the tour, replaced by Johnny Marr.

That circumstance hasn't befallen this fivesome, yet an aura emanates. They can feel it, a strength, people in time, alchemy, they almost certainly won't be partners long enough for infighting, or acrimony. There will be creativity and cohesion, a band leader (Kate), a pecking order, Kate, Django, Max, Geoff, then Foto-ace, and camaraderie. For now it's all Django's got.

The youthful Barrister's Clerk has an obsequious plastered smile, he's snuck discretely from the glass doors, so that they can't be penetrated without him returning with the keycode. He is classically attired, pinstripe, clean-cut, enthusiastic, lard face,

climbing the greasy to the silks. The five look, expectant, the two

newsmen, a rummy combination of bemused and belligerent, Kate,

authoritarian, Geoff, pensive, Django, ambivalent.

"It's just… Sorry to keep you."

Kate stands, "That's alright."

He avoids her eyes, focusing on the cups on the table, as if he's

going to wash them up, in-fact, the last job he'd ever do. The clerk

is treading glass splinters, unable to conceal his reluctance to

ruminate the words he's been instructed to say.

"It's just, Mr. and Mrs. Henderson won't have the two reporters in."

Kate unexpectedly puts her arm over the lad's shoulders, taking him

completely off guard, and the telephone-dolly upturns her head from

the switchboard in surprise. Kate says, friendly, smiling, continually

moving him in the direction of the entrance from whence he

emerged, her face so close to his, he can smell her perfume, and the

coffee from her breath, "They're advisers, so we'll need them there,

Mr. Biancho and his lawyer, Mr. Thomas have checked it out, it's all

alright." The assistant tries to butt in, but Kate has the lead-card, as

he can't exactly obstruct their entry now, at the gateway. She continues bullshitting to get to the threshold, "It's integral…" Max and the rest follow, knowing completely what Kate is up to, playing their role. She is the Malcolm McClaren of the situation, they're going in. The telephonic-poodle is ineffective and gawps at the audacity. It's what got Kate into Generation X backstage party at Hammersmith Odeon on the night Billy Idol departed in a Limo for solo stardom and the rest of the band were forced to get the bus home, and countless gigs, record company soirées, and music paper Christmas parties. It's an 'exodus for the people', as Django would refer to it, in the future. The bemused two's smirks turn to grins, Geoff keeps close to Django, they bunch up at the doorway, Kate helps him with the keycode, and they're in the temple.

In one minute they crowd QC Hutchinson's chambers. It is too small for Robin Hutchinson, Dr. Richard, Eileen and William, their solicitor Philip Yudson, Kate, Django, Geoff, Max and Foto-ace. The secretary has yet to come in to take notes. The Henderson's and their brief have lost the will to evict the reporters. It seems surly, un-English. Kate was counting on this. She is receiving a five figure sum for Django, plus hotel, expenses, legal costs, and various emollients. The correspondents have to play tag. Kate's gothiness is toned, and shoulder-padding has worked its way into her jacket. Eileen's dusted-off Channel trouser suit was flattering and trendy when she was thirty. It now looks like she's lined it with mdf. William could easily be going directly to his office in 1975, après meeting.

Max presses the record button on the Olympus recorder inside his rainmac pocket whilst people are distracted by seating disorder. Hutchinson is behind his desk, more through necessity than choice, as the room is chocka. The desk is accommodated like a primary school art class, everybody looking in, Hutchinson, Yudson, Eileen, William, Kate, and Django. The supporting players on the periphery. The panelled walls house legal reference tomes, framed certificates, and family photos. The desk-phone buzzes, Hutchinson lifts the receiver, "No more calls Jane please." He is in his forties, a scampish Adam Faith blonde mien, which seems lightweight for someone of his seniority. This is what he uses to disarm opponents, sneaking up on them in court. It gives him an unparalleled and expensive reputation. He's in a plain, hand-made, lot. Hutchinson, at last, "Perhaps there's a middle ground, the family court Judge would expect mediation before it ever gets to court, we could bypass that, and save a lot of expense Miss Kingston, Mr. Biancho, if we can…. Isn't that correct Mr. Thomas?" Geoff has no idea, and answers accordingly, "Yes." Kate glares at him, he's wrong-footed. Eileen is fit to burst, she rises, as if addressing a charity golfing auction, making sure her jacket has no crumples. A wisp of sun strikes the table from the narrow window behind Hutchinson, which captures the action in a small private courtyard behind the building. An immaculate setting, two well-groomed lawns coupled by a central slate path leading to a patio, decked with pot plants, and a couple of wooden benches, where the secretaries munchtime sandwiches, grab a ciggy, and raise the chambers' gossip column. It's hemmed in by old brick walls, punctuated with established and pruned clematis, and wild roses. "Your reporter pals note this," Eileen proceeds with her completely predictable speech, a lecture they'd been expecting, even hoped for, as it gives their case legs. Hutchinson, William, and Yudson suffer it like a public school speech from a dull alumnus, who now traverses mountains for a living, during a lengthy dinner, enriched with large portions of mashed potato and over-boiled runner beans. They sigh and look disconsolate, and wonder why they're there. It's all trolled out,

'Good for nothing', and

'Drug addicts', and

'Never had a job', and

'Ruined my daughter', and

'Ruined our lives', and

'Poor baby needs care and the best treatment', and

'Mr. Biancho is this and that and the other', and

'We'll use every means', and

'Mr. Biancho doesn't have a hope of winning', and

'We'll use every penny', and so it drones on. Kate's bored, knowing the meeting's over. She's got what she needed.

Kate stands, "Let's go, Mr. Thomas will be in touch." Mr. Thomas is taken off guard, as he's diligently been writing Eileen's words, and he jolts a bit. Hutchinson has the balls to do the right thing, "Mr. Thomas, please hang back, you and I and Mr. Yudson can discuss the next stage." Kate, "No, they'll be none of that, everybody out." She bookends Hutchinson, not in the least bit

intimidated by the setting, its history, its close proximity to the law,

courts, power, and cloaked, be-wigged officials that decide how you

and I rummage about in our world.

"We'll be in touch, they'll be a court order."

"The next stage is.... the court procedure is -" Hutchinson knows the

protocol but before he can finish, Kate has assembled her mob out

the door. They'd spent longer finding chairs and getting seated, than

they had discussing ConeBoy's future.

Foto-ace hangs about and gets clandestine photographs of

Eileen and William leaving, thirty minutes later, with Dr. Richard

and Yudson. He decamps to Maison Rouge, next to Whistles in

Covent Garden, where Kate is giving her best shot at a de-brief. It's

that juncture between lunch and dinner, about 3 pm, when people

who've had errands in the morning, or have appointments in the

evening, jostle with time. It seems wrong to stare at the television,

or make a trivial leisure pursuit, like playing tennis at the public

courts in Battersea Park, or drinking with the winos in a pub just off

Tottenham Court Road, when everyone else is working. People like

Kate and Django resist these hours, they've become used to stinking

them up with doo-doo, dousing them with lighter fuel, and riding

time's motorbike into a wall of death. They can fill it up with stuff,

and that's what they're doing. Kate would turn it into an art, a

career. It's a knack, keep on talking, keep on fiddling, then suddenly

there's coalescence, where, before it was cake-mix powder. Kate's

paying anyway, so they stay sat, Max listening, soaking it up, and

Django is ringing his orange juice glass with the tip of his forefinger.

Maison Rouge is just that, a red pseudo French country

house, as the English would like to imagine. It's another nine years

until 'A Year in Provence' has an impact. It'd be no surprise if the

head chef popped out from the kitchens on his French Onion Seller's

Bike, stripy top, beret, long twists of onions hanging from his

handlebars. Except the nearest this place gets to French is the tat

picked up from an Aquitaine flea-market strung around amid

tantalising wall-size black and white Jean-Luc-Godard modish

photographs, papering every inch. The bench seats are blood-red

velour, against brass coloured wood mouldings, to suit the nom de

plume, lighting dimmed to reduce dusting. The food is bog eighties action, printing it straight to large digital Betacam cassettes, to be replayed in numerous evening reports and ten o'clock news slots. Kate made sure the timing of the hearing would extract maximum evening exposure, after all, it was Bill Grundy at tea time who broke the Sex Pistols. Eileen and William won't be seen, they've flown the roost at the rear, ala 'Elvis has left the building' via Carey Street. Even Foto-ace has missed his break to catch them draining out the back, he's so caught up in the hype. A carefully worded statement relayed by Yudson is announced in each news slot, to give journalistic balance, though everyone knew Django was going to win. There is talk of an 'appeal', 'injustice', 'what's best for ConeBoy', etc. The Grandparents disappear from view, devastated, for the second time. The be-wigged one has advised that ConeBoy should have visitation with his Grandparents, but the court doesn't have the power to grant access rights to them, it just doesn't exist in law, and he's not setting any precedents today, 5th March 1981. Afternoon strollers, workers and tourists peer from over the road, and the commotion in front of the Gothic building resembles a pack of rabid starving wolves rampaging a deer they've brought down, only, lit with BBC portable studio lamps. The solid George Edmund

Street building remains indifferent, self-effacing, it has no opinion, or if it has, it would be slight cynicism, it's seen many court-post-coital celebrations, knowingly eyeing the proceedings, each winner must also bolt a bitter pill, leading to post-success-depression. People are in court because of a deeper seated tribulation. Success has its price. The grey stone edifice rises proudly above the dense mangled animals, its vast clock face shaped Portland stone rose window stolidly un-moved by the debacle, elegantly sweeping up to the perfectly geometric lofty polygon spire.

Opposite, there's commotion. A few of the fan-club distracted, a Mercedes-Benz T2 long wheel-base van, jet-black, with blacked out cargo windows has parked up beside the news vehicles and cabs, blocking their vision, and obstructing the carriageway, buses arrested. A man with rapier legs, scarcely a lump of flesh on his long Cuban-heeled frame, dressed black head-to-toe, like the devil, flings himself up on to the roof from the driver's seat, using it as a sort of trampoline-cum-ladder to spring up on top. He removes his hat and waves it, catching the attention of the police. The Reich cap's silver badge reflects the sun, and he screams at the top of his to his Mum, who's at the table with her back to them. Gash is facing Django and Colin, legs astride, hands in pockets, "Hello little man!" Elsbeth keeps her compose, slugging a fourth drink. She is wearing the same mini-dress from court, and the grey sports top she's had for years, except she has ripped off the collar, so it slinks over one shoulder, at an angle, exposing her cleavage, and the top of one breast, just above the nipple. Her hair is longer, dyed bright blond, volumised by clumps pinned up behind each ear. She has bare legs, and new black suede pixie boots, with a slight heel. "Els', Elsbeth," Django tentatively articulates. Gash is looking at Elsbeth, awaiting her reply. Django repeats, "Elsbeth, Eslie," to no reaction. She drinks. "Else, why is he here? I thought we'd? - " She twists on her pixies, a rigid twirl, and answers, sinewy, and out-of-character, between her teeth, "I can't," she slumps past Django, brushing him, "get me some fuckin' coke," and heads for the group she recognises as being acquaintances. Django looks to Gash, and Gash offers, "Want me to take him home?" Colin is bored, and starts to pull at the white tablecloth V hanging in front of him.

"No thanks, I'm taking this off, it's not right, I don't know why she -
"

"Yeah whatever man."

Django's black Tux trousers are mucked up, so it doesn't matter that
he kneels for the second time.

"I'm just taking off your hat Col', watch your cone."

He answers in his chirpy nasal grate, "Daddy, can I have a drink
Daddy, orange juice Daddy?"

Colin reaches up for the cartons on the top, that are untouched, and
Django slides the veil up, slowly, avoiding friction. He folds the silk
shroud into his suit jacket pocket, and there is an audible gasp. The
phlegm promulgates as sick for two individuals.

The door-rugs are taken off guard by the side-show child,
when three motorbikes pull-up outside in the empty alley, and the
pillion riders dismount. Ali walks in with them, wearing one of his
decidedly popular designs that has caught the zeitgeist, under a plain
black jacket, and black jeans, unequivocally smarter, is late, due to a
distribution deal meeting, and is the only one confronted by Ginger
and Scott, as he's so reluctant to cross the threshold, even though he
has an invite tucked in a gap somewhere. The others have the
swagger, and easily gatecrash. The three twenty year olds are

dressed like Nick Kamen and start taking photographs, but not of the art. Gash is the first to react, then Ginger, then Ali, but the snappers have what they need by the time they're banished, and the other attendees can't wait to leave. ConeBoy's delighted and runs about, bumping off the white metal pillars, he seldom has a chance to let loose anywhere, and it's a great big playroom full of colourful pictures, and people he trusts. Ali, Gash, Scott and Ginger stare embarrassed, as Elsbeth projects accusation at Django, and he fails to react with anger. Scott and Ginger retreat with a couple of bottles each, they didn't sign up for this. Django composedly responds, but Elsbeth counterpoints each soporific reply with a bitter, tired, tetherless retort.

"It's nobody's fault."

"It's your fault, they found the blood, the fuckin' blood line, whatever it's called."

"Don't Elsbeth, how could I have known."

"You should have fuckin' known your family are mutants before putting your dick in me."

"Don't be ridiculous, they didn't find..."

"Oh yeah?! What about your Mum and Dad being brother and

sister, that little gem would have been useful would it?!!"

Elsbeth screams, and her gums show, they're receding and she looks long-in-the-tooth.

"I'm not staying at home with him all day unless you get me coke!"

"C'mon, you're scaring Colin."

ConeBoy has stopped running, and is holding on to a pillar, slowly rotating. Ali has gone over to see to him, and put himself between the warring pair and their offspring, in an attempt to mollify the battle.

Elsbeth pulls the snood from Django's jacket pocket, goes to ConeBoy, carefully puts it over the mass of grist, takes his hand, gets her breath, "C'mon Ali, give me a hand please." Ali shrugs his shoulders, "I'll see ya later Djang', Gash," and leaves with Elsbeth and ConeBoy.

In the empty room Gash and Django lay on the floor in the corner by the Snow Angel. The music is still ringing, and Gash has put The Stooges on. Both have a bottle of champagne, dishevelled, they're a little inebriated, Django smoking, and Gash with his roll-up, picking at the edge of the Brut label. Django is at the bottom of can get through this. Cue camera six!" Parfitt and Rossi's pressed denims suit the audience, not too risqué, a jean jacket waistcoat here, a drummer with a forehead sweat band there, a hint at their rock 'n' roll past, and a dribble of hope for Radio Two playlisting. The displays exhibit the ageing rockers, legs apart, Chuck Berry fifths and sevenths shaped up on the Telecasters, miming to an easily forgotten late career coffin. Producer man is eyeing Titchmarsh from the non-live feed, both know what's coming, producer man is sick in his stomach, as are the women, both now dragging on Embassy No.10's, equally jittery. "Here we go, cue camera one, and CUT!" ConeBoy enters from the corner as the last chords ring from the studio PA speakers, audience appreciation quickly diminishing. "Camera two, let's get close up, just the face, is it a face, close in, that's it, and cue camera TWO!" In the tiered seating, resembling a musty village hall and depressed ice-rink, a couple of the old-dears have fainted, and it's not from seeing their heroes Parfitt and Rossi. There is hushed panic as the floor manager and runners get the bodies out. Other audience members turn aside, and the queasier are sick into hankies, or whatever is to hand. Suddenly the gallery, above the proceedings is a hub of unwelcome activity, phones ringing, and unwanted bodies entering, despite the red warning light over the door outside. Producer man holds his own, an ability to argue, and juggle what a nation of lunch-time viewers are allowed to see on live TV, his chosen skill, "I didn't fuckin' book him, I fuckin' told them, fuckin' Birtey had a memo, they fuckin' ignored it." The life size cranium is filling the screen, as if a surrealist artist had defecated on a teenager's face, oozed it around with his fingers, carefully blotching in the impression of a huge pussy fly, then pressed a large chromed rocket ship exhaust pipe in the middle. The physiognomy judders as it breaths like jello with a giant multi-legged isopod buried within, attempting to constantly suck up life. Titchmarsh is gripping the sides of his anchorman easy chair, his thumbs imprinting a trench in the leather arms.

Cramps for millennials, even recruiting a Poison Ivy, Link Wray sound-alike, who twangs a massive Gretsch 6120 hollow body and Fender twin, with the reverb springs turned up to full, over a Suicide TR606 electro beat that went out with Acid House. It's lost on a Blink 182 and Snow Patrol world and Pauli is back-sliding like a million aspirers before him. Soon he'll be home in Redcar. Elsbeth is living-out her Nico and John Cooper Clarke, John and Yoko, Sid and Nancy, Kurt Cobain and Courtney Love phase, with him. Except neither have any talent. The other anomaly, is, she loves drugs, and not the man, if you could call him a man. At forty-eight she can still do the business in the 'get-up' department, the gravitational pull that causes husband-stray hasn't yet kicked-in, but she is on the verge. It's core to her, since she wants to look sexy for a boy who is a few years older than her son. He's waiting patiently, shirtless, his yellow and black striped Steven Tyler silk stage-scarf tied on his wrist, hugging black jeans, and bare feet. She has the gear out on the futon, crack mixed with Ecstasy and Temazepam, and the needle they're sharing pulling back off a heated silver spoon, gurgling from the Zippo she's fixedly roasting it with. She's irresistible, Elsbeth dexterously manages to make drug abuse sexy, as she loves it. Lifestyle, equipment, the outcastes it attracts, skitting societal norms her bedrock. She tourniquets his arm, extends it, "Now baby," he looks in her eyes, and she administers him, then the same for herself. The opiates lengthen the euphoria, they need it, such is the addiction to the stimulus they'll repeat this several times during the night. The effect on Pauli is immediate, he pulls off his jeans, he is a long rake, a marathon runner minus the obsessive compulsive disorder. He has no underwear and pushes the tight ankles off on to the floor, his feet are filthy, nails encrusted with scuz. Pauli's penis is erect, but Elsbeth hasn't noticed yet, she'll have sex in a tick. For the moment she's breathing deeply, rolling her head back, eyes closed, similarly fuzzed hair, riven with split ends shaken out over her shoulders. She slunks, tartan Vivienne Westward imitation dress rucks-up, her thighs revealed as having scraggy spare flesh hanging, lacking tone. She rolls one leg over on to him and caresses his penis plunging to his genitalia. She has her pixie boots on, and on one, the sole has come unglued, her big-toe exposed. Her finger nails are long, not the elegant strain, but the cop-out category. They are yellowing, and dirt is ingrained between the cuticles and their nail bed. Just before she commits to fellatio, curtain-twitch, making a mental note of the comings and goings of Saudis, Russians, Americans, Asians, and the one pop star who lives in the road. Gash is noticeably pincered, the roll-up's reduced, the speed thrown to the mists of time. He can't quite kick the rolling up and prepping with the tin, papers, and shag, to the constant consternation of his partner. It's seen him suffer one minor stroke, a bunch of tests and angiogram, the stint in hospital shaking them both up. Blister packs of pills in the bathroom keep it at bay. Gash's arm is stretched across the radiator top, resting on a four inch wide piece of wood, which Django especially made, to stop Gash's arm dropping in the gap between the radiator's two panels, and creating indents in his forearms from perpetual sitting. This way he can keep his arm comfortable, to intermittently flick ash in to the saucer beside his hand. He'd sit there permanently if it wasn't for meals, and errands. Gash has become boney in direct proportion to Django's plumping. Above his narrow lips are wizened vertical smoker's lines, small crabby wrinkles, and his icy blue eyes protrusiveness is accentuated by his Bez spindling. Gash has on his Alice Cooper jacket, picked up off the stage at the end of a gruelling drug infused tour, before Cooper traded in his crack cocaine dependency for golf-clubs. It's his pride and joy, hand-tailored, the arms are stitched to simulate motorbike-wear stretch panels, and the Japanese leather, soft and lightweight enough to wear like a sweatshirt throughout the day. The black jeans no longer arrest circulation, but are shaped enough to demonstrate Gash's rock 'n' roll inclination. The Cubans have given vent to John Richmond leather sneakers. Underneath the jacket is a white t-shirt, forevermore the same, plain, picked up on Ventura, when he's there. His non smoking hand is tucked in his waist, thumb behind a black leather belt, with Motorhead buckle, "That's a Russian car, Russian plates, you wonder why they go to the trouble of shipping it over, when they could easily buy one here. There's a Lamborghini dealer on the block." Django glances from his doodling, "Probably bullet proofed." They laugh wildly as if an in-joke only they get. Django is pre-occupied by his drawing, popping his head up to recalibrate his subject now and then. He uses the A1 blotting sheets that Gash buys him, and the sharpie pens that sit in a large tupperware on his desk. The effect is one of creeping fountain pen ink on absorbent kitchen roll, but with some structure. It's not serious, he likes to compose in-between phone calls and paperwork, and the material's delineation suits his florid daubings. Swaubs of concentric oval neons house a corroded face, the features muffled and smudged, except for a stark profiled Bauhaus'ian linear pyramid dead-centre, as if welded together from RSJ's. It whines in its snouting spoilt tone from the chaises-longue, "I'm doing nothing beyond Christmas, nothing for 2002." Django returns his fish-eye to the subject and it's in its best resting position, the Conran C-shaped recliner cradles its constantly fatigued shoulders and neck, the padded leather headrest allowing just the right amount of tilt for the Proteus protuberance. It reaches out, and takes the oxygen mask, and places it over its orifices, turns the tap, and the mechanistics blur out the Archers in the background, from the radio that is on in the kitchen. It leans in a little toward the tank to get the best hit, allowing the pipes within its soft tissue malformations to open as wide as possible. The chair is revealed as pony skin, but a little stained from lesions that it's hiding. "Let's get that cleaned again shall we, and get the nurse up to look at those?" says Django, Gash, still down the road apiece, replies, "Don't worry, I'll do it." Django dashes large exploratory ovals, like ostentatious Ostrich eggs, "Don't spend too long on that Colin, it's not meant for that," the daily reprimanding a waste-ofwheeze. It takes a long suck in, Django and Gash tag the regularity, like the chimes of Big Ben, because it annoyingly waits for the nostril contraption click, when one flap descends and the other rises, before pulling the mask off, and hanging it back on the cylinder. It shuts the bottle's valve, "I mean it Daddy." Django swivels in the coordinated Conran office chair to view the Sasco Year Planner up behind him. A mass of multi-coloured drywipe marker entries, it's the same battle Django has with it everyday, he just needs to re-tone the inducement, "I don't mind, you know what it means though?" It's furious, and uses its unnatural cavities and frontal horn to blast orders.

"Where's Granny's money!!"

"You know you get it next year. It's all in trusts, I've got no control, in any case, you can't spend it on sweet FA, except basics, they'll see to that. Don't you think I've tried? Most of it went on the court case."

"And that's you!! You idiot bastard!! What was the point of all that!!"

Django turns and looks at it, lifts a pile of invoices and solicitors letters off the desk, talks placidly, "Your little weekend has cost a

CHAPTER 21 - FLAME HAIR GIRL

The hearing is kept secret, but a few journalists have worked it out. Diligent commanders of the Intellectual Property courts at Rolls Building, Fetter Lane are more accustomed to cloaked barristers and suited juniors drubbing it out over copyrights and patents. A minion is tasked with scanning the litigants list every week at The Telegraph, and a couple of other papers that can be bothered with the chore, to see who is suing who. They registered the ConeBoy trademark, and Dgango couldn't bar them. A gaggle at the doors, and a small crowd in the reception, who are briskly evicted. Judge Hacon has issued instructions for the behaviour of the whole court, recognising it could become a circus, if it wasn't so already. The train's come off the track, the golden goose is cooked, and its eggs omletted, with Italian seasoning. No-one knows what's going on. Django is fighting a sicko ideal, ready to bankrupt himself and Gash, entreaties from the Gashdom, falling on deaf ears. The website has a 'temporarily under maintenance' notice, so sales have halted, personal appearances postponed, and more damaging, the commitment to television has tailed off. Coneboy has persuaded a strong-willed west-end lawyer no-win-no-fee, and Django is representing himself, so sure is he of his defence. It's not a space for the queasy. A rainy depressed October Wednesday afternoon, the outlook typifying the sorrow unfolding, the blind lead the blind, into a disconcerting tangle, where emotions, protection, devotion, power, money, and misaligned principles mutate, and are disfigured like a two headed monster. The Judge is a better man if he can fathom it out.

I was ready to do the tour. Imagine, fifty dates across the USA, the Christian Fundamentalists out protesting in force at every college, banners, placards, public TV, cable channels, internet, national TV, then the girls. There would be girls, those American chicks are crazy, they'd fuck anything, including me. It was a holocaust in waiting; The Sex Pistols at Winterland, except I was sad Sid, the scapegoat, the dork who could only play one note, then change it, when Steve Jones said. Nevertheless, I was ready, I lanked around Soho that afternoon, and for two days, went to some clubs, which I was thrown out of, even Groucho's, who normally allow any scum in, then Gash took me home, drunk, and stoned.

JOHNNO. The nail in the coffin, when I was certain none of it was

in my interests. Daddy thought he was doing the right things, I

guess, he got caught up. Like one Elvis film too many, one Paul

McCartney and Elvis Costello collaboration too much, one Big

Country album too far. He lost the thread.

I didn't want to do it, I'm not in the least musical, and La

Monte Young wasn't the right influence for this kind of endeavour.

Johnno turns up, I didn't know him, and it's like the old days for the

four. You know how it is, the rose tinted spectacles were out. I was

impressed that Daddy and Mummy might get back together, such

was the jollity. Then the slammer. Johnno used £500 Daddy gave

him, apparently, to start his own studio, Bombardier Sounds, and a

label, just reggae and dub acts, and he was bringing bands over to

gig, putting them up, recording them, and sticking out acetates and

dub-plates. You know, hawking them to venues, and record stores,

maybe selling two hundred or so if lucky. Then he records this song,

'My Girl's Giddyup', you've heard it. What it is, the deals were; he

had the publishing, and production rights, as the bands didn't pay

any studio costs, so he had what they call now, a three-hundred-and-sixty-degree deal. He wanted to pay Daddy back, plus interest, but Daddy wasn't having any of it. They cooked up a drunken spliff-squiffy idea that I could do a record, and sell it exclusively on the website, for a laugh, limited edition, and signed copies, at £50. I said no, but the music came over by courier, a backing track on a CD, with a demo vocal by Johnno, they only needed me there for an hour, to sample my voice, then synthesisers and harmonisers would do the magic. I sounded like a visceral Steven Hawking brawling with Cher on 'Believe', and it climbed the charts. 'Finir'.

Everyone is early, even Elsbeth. No-one has the mettle for it, wishing it would disappear, especially Elsbeth, who's life had waxed and waned through media, courts, scrutiny. She dreams now, more than anyone, to settle, with a guy about eleven years younger than her, an artist, musician, or even an artisan, maybe someone who could use their hands, a carpenter, or baker. They'd get a bit messed up every evening, on bottles of strong cider, mushrooms, possibly LSD, put on a Wishbone Ash or Spirit album, and jig around their tiny Canterbury cottage sitting room. The cameras are straight on her, her cab chucking her out right in front of the court building, her oval sunglasses needing windscreen wipers in the torrent of rain.

Gash knows the score, he's got his cab to stop at Bream's Buildings,

he and Django leg it, hiding themselves, the element of surprise.

The weather's beating, and there is no shelter at Fetter Lane, the

sheer vertical aluminium and glass offices provide no protection.

They'd forgotten a brolly, so Django has to run with his briefcase

under his coat. He is perspiring, and soaking by the time they get to

security, and the hold up there creates the perfect opportunity for the

reporters. 'Django! Django! Where's the money Django?!

Shouldn't ConeBoy be a millionaire? Haven't you stolen your son's

money Mr. Biancho? Are you stealing your son's name?' and the

cameras get him at his worst.

ConeBoy is prepared, a veteran, he knows how to manipulate

the press, something happened along the way, and he has a bunch of

thirty second sound-bites. Half a mile from the court, they graze

Holborn, in the black-taxi, with Amanda Redmond, the barrister, and

Russell Davis the lawyer accompanying him. They've picked him

up from a flat in Surrey Quays, ConeBoy having had the tenacity to

call Max, who has sided with the boy (for the story), and put him up in one of Mirror Group's properties. Max doesn't see much in the narrative, but feels for the kid, and it's low budget. There's no Mirror journo's there, Max has organised an exclusive filming for their website later, after the verdict. ConeBoy's heart is beating up in his chest, breathing heavy, he's regulating his cone, the window is open, his cover is getting wet, but he needs the oxygen. Redmond is reading from the papers, an expansive box folder opened out on her knees. She knows this is a career changer, and she's revising like a sixth-former. She's meticulously pieced together bank accounts, trails of finance, a nest of Limited Companies, contracts, implied contracts, and the thorny and tangled 'use of name' concern, over months. They lurch the corner, the flashes start before he's out of the vehicle. Davis leans and stuffs a £50 note through the dividing glass, panicking, not getting his change from the cabbie. ConeBoy reveals his head, his pulse racing a hundred miles per hour, the crisp Armani shirt and suit sweating up, his familiar repugnant odour bursting forth over the ton of armour plated anti-perpsirant, and Paco Rabbane. The brow is seen first, the crusty malignant tumour like a wholemeal loaf risen with too much yeast, some bony mass criss-crossing. It's grown as he's matured, they said it would, a host of can feel, kisses him all over his face, so hard so he knows she is kissing him, all the while embracing. Davis is there at the stairs with two plastic cups of water, and Redmond is equal with him, they catch each other's faces, confused, mystified. Elsbeth gently pulls back, her arms running down his, feeling the bamboo band as they part. She hauls up using her haunches, letting him go. He's silent. Elsbeth takes her coat and bag, and goes round the corner to the lift. An office boy gets out, she enters, the door closes, and she's gone.

"His Right Honourable Judge Hacon," the deputy announces, everyone stands. Hacon is slightly younger than Django, grey hair tidily swept back, a smiling face that calms the nervy atmosphere in the room. He wears a smart day-suit, is high up, about three metres above his minions, the court especially constructed to show who's in charge. A huge one metre wide royal coat of arms is behind him, lion to the left, horse on right, the inscription running below, Dieu et mon Droit, which Django can't avert his eyes from. There is a skylight window strip, near the ceiling, that requires a long screw jack opener. The threaded rod is leaned upright in the corner, redundant, the air conditioning having replaced it. It's the only link with the great outdoors, and the rain has cleared, blue sky poking

through. It's gone well for Django and he's buoyant. They've been

given a thirty minute break, so Hacon can go and flesh out his

summing up. He knows he'll be quoted in a number of Law

Journals, and in student syllabuses, case IP 7591717065-A, Biancho

v Biancho, for many years hence, he can't get a letter wrong.

Hacon's seated, they follow. A long bar table houses both the

defence and plaintiff, facing the Judge, Django and Gash on the left.

Between them, at ground level is the Judge's associate, managing the

recording devices, and ensuring no one breaks the barrier. Django

has a mess of notes splayed in front of him, also fed by Gash, who

has been allowed as the McKenzie friend, and thus barred as

witness. Django made a long winding statement, shuffling his

papers, and the Judge asked him numerous questions in a

sympathetic and charitable manner. Redmond was allowed her bit,

and Django felt he'd shined under attack, arguing everything he'd

done had been for the benefit of his boy. Django went for the break

complimenting himself to Gash. They sat drinking machine tea

Django wouldn't normally touch with a bargepole, and he couldn't

stop asking Gash how it went, then saying, "It went well didn't it?"

list in my bag for you. Are you a proper doctor Mr. Menglees? You know, your website -" Menglees looks ConeBoy straight on ignoring the road, "Up in Canada. You can take that gear off kid, the bag, I'll be seeing a lot of you, you can take it off in the car, let people see, it's no problem." ConeBoy is concentrating on the rumination of billboards clustered along the highway, "If it seems I am dropping off to sleep, wake me up, there is this contraption in my luggage, it assembles, it was made, it stops my oesophagus being crushed. It's not usually a problem, see, I am on various drugs, they keep me awake, but the jet-lag, I'm not used to the -" Menglees leans across the bench seat slightly and slaps ConeBoy on the leg, "Stop worrying kid, you're staying with us, you'll be fine."

"Staying with you?"

Menglees is now looking for his exit, "Yeah, Irena and me, we have room ready, at home." ConeBoy is feeling the strain, his heart sinking into his Nike trainers, "I thought it was a hospital, Birkenhead Heights."

"Yeah, Yeah, Birkenhead, it's a facility, we rent the facility, it's the best, don't worry kid, you're booked in, tests start Wednesday morning, eight in the morning, day after tomorrow, one day to get over the flight. I rent space there, like a bunch of specialists, there's a group of us, it'll be fine kid, don't worry, I specialise in physical abnormalities. You're going to be worried, it's the best, nurses, equipment, the works, don't worry kid, I've done all this, in Poland, Brazil, we've just got to sort out the balance, the rest of the money kid."

There are eighteen caravans, static, in the general area, that at one time housed a playground, and recreational hinterland for the Brunel Estate in Rotherhithe. From above, it sits directly over the Tunnel entrance, the 1960's brick built block would be an exact rectangle, except one side was partly rubbed out by a 'visionary' planner to only allow access for pedestrians. The resultant lack of surveillance, for residents' cars parked in surrounding streets, created the crime hotspot that's eroded the community. The municipal kiddie's swings and slides have been manhandled out of the ground by the traveller fraternity and hauled off to the scrappies, in Ilderton Road, tucked behind Millwall. There was just enough room at the estate's entrance to squeeze a caravan through, and gypsies took the initiative. White Transits with 'Motorway

Maintenance' stick-on transfers, and yellow-red chevrons praying skyward, splashed across the rear doors, and magnetic yellow beacons on the roofs, the twelve volt wire trailed in the window to the cigarette lighter, buddy the trailers. 'Asphalt' and 'Tarmac' with mobile phone numbers sign-written on the sides. There are a few new Mercedes, and pick-up trucks. The immaculateness of the mobile homes is not reflected in the surroundings. About a year's worth of house clearances, unwanted rubbish from roadway jobs, dumped fridges, cookers, burnt out vehicles, and household refuse demonstrate the fragile and collegial relationship the traveller community embrace, with their environment. Human waste from chemical toilets is poured into open drains intended for surface water run-off, which are now backed-up, and the stench is bordering choleric. It is a dangerous, and intimidating place in the day. At night it's a free-for-all hell-hole. Even the filthy toddlers that roam amongst the detritus are worrying.

Elsbeth enters, and closely edges the sides, the penumbra that would have been the tiny garden fronts of the ground floor residences, a balcony walkway for the flats above disallowing any worthwhile cultivation. Doors are broken-in, because cable and copper piping has been stripped and sold-on. Elsbeth has her hand on a rape-spray in her bag, her frame bent. The natives aren't interested, they've seen her before. The freezing December weather has no effect on the men, they're hanging out in clusters around burning fire-pits, smoking, and clacking an indecipherable cant, in vests and t-shirts. There's moronic cat-calls from them, "A'right luv!" and two horrid ten year olds make themselves even more dislikeable, following her, throwing a slew of thick-arse questions in that cheerful yet threatening manner that itinerant off-spring manage so well. Elsbeth is in a long black thick wool trench coat that she has half-inched from a boyfriend, and it wholly disguises her figure, and everything else she's wearing. Only black calf-length boots can be seen. A black woollen hat is pulled right below her ears, long scraggy hair billowing in the cold wind that is siphoned into the quadrangle, courtesy of the innovative Swedish blueprint. She enters the first stairwell she comes to, as she can circumnavigate the walkways above, to reach her destination, rather than contending with the spume below. The kids get bored, as they know where she's going, and mug off to dent a washing machine with a rusty metal railing for an hour. She bangs on thirty-five, the fifth floor, whilst eyeing the inbreds. It's the only surviving door on the block, and has been reinforced with metal plate outside, and metal bars covering the door-frame on the lock side. In reality, it could be smashed in easily but the nomads can't be bothered. The windows on either side have been boarded with off-cuts of chipboard and OSB. In the time it would take a couple of Irish roamers to break in, she is lying on a squalid fabric of bedding on the floor in what used to be the living room, having intercourse with the drummer from The Cuddly Toys. Beside her, the window and door to the rear is planked over, to stop balcony hopping, and entry to the flat. One of the panes must be smashed, as there is a draft coming in. Candles are not a particular purchase priority for the dwellers, a solitary one, sitting centre, on a broken saucer that also doubles as an ash-tray, and which is full to overflowing. Various states of stupor clamp the other six junkies in position, three crammed on the seedy sofa which is flat up against a wall, and three spread about the floor on scummy cushions, blankets, and one flea-bitten mattress. Drug paraphernalia is everywhere; finished plastic two litre containers of Diamond White, and emptied quart bottles of meths. There are tubes of glue, but it's a trifle, an hors d'oeuvre, a 'bit-of-a-laugh', a bauble to the main-course for the benumbed. "That's alright Paddy, I'll bring you off later baby," she breathes in his ear. There's no reason for her undertone, or to hide, as no-one is particularly interested. He is panting in her ear, has lost his erection, if it could ever have been called that in the first instance. She is still completely dressed, be-coated, supine, him on top. She has opened her legs, and he has gone at her, hoping for some redemption in the manhood department. Jacking up in his groin to get speedier and more efficient drug infusions to his bloodstream, hasn't helped in that department. He rolls off and she yanks his member in a tried and trusted teat milking agitation, to no avail. Elsbeth sidles her panties in to place, and pulls the coat right over, leaning up on her side facing him. There is a dark thin atmosphere in the room, it's not very large, the flat would have housed an elderly couple, or single parent with one child. A fireplace has been relieved of its gas burner, and the back boiler that was installed behind it (from refurbishments in the 1970's). The iron burners of the boiler are valuable scrap, and have been looted. Floorboards are burning apathetically in the remaining gap, crowbarred from the other flats, and rooms. The Asbestolux cowling that blocked the old chimneys as part of the re-fit has been smashed out. Fifty per-cent of the smoke blows-in, the wood gives of little heat, it's freezing and lacking ventilation. Paddy's bald at the front of his head, and his bright red Crazy-Colour mop commences about half way on his skull. What's lacking in front is made up for at the rear. Elsbeth pats him on the chest. His shirt is open, he is hot, from effort, for the moment. The shirt is bright red and matches his hair. Ribs stipple his chest, his lungs heave, he gets his breath. His sturdy torso is from drumming, or so he likes to think. He is deluded, as he hasn't seen the back of a drum kit since 1997, when Cuddly Toys toppled out of their nondescript existence. He had a short disastrous stint with Johnny Thunders, unceremoniously ejected from the back of the van on the closing leg of a godawful UK tour. Paddy's continued with the drummer ruse, it's a good excuse. And what's wrong with that? He's done his hurting, like the rest of these human-beings scrabbling in here at the tail end of their rickety turbid lives. Parents stolen from, girlfriends, boyfriends, wives, and husbands betrayed, children abandoned, friends deceived, ambitions squandered until there's no going back, they are where they are, they know what they are, they embrace what they are, it's relished, and who is on the moral high ground? Who is to say what's wrong and what's right? They are free in the world to do their preference, to rock their boat, to sail their ship. They're not hurting anyone, they're not bombing children in Syria. One could argue they're part of a 'bigger problem', a 'malaise', a 'contemporary disease', a 'drug pandemic' they're central to, promoting by default. It's cascaded to children, crack sold outside schools, kids enticed to skunk, thirteen year old pushers separated by streets, being murdered for turf, only to be replaced by another. In this second, they're hurting themselves, choices made, a superficial code bonds them, that which they can amplify their dreams, turbo-charge their self-consciousness, tap into the dusky dormant atoms, to get high for an instant, the slow-slaughter by needle. "Let's do it darling," Elsbeth indicates to his concoction which he has stashed in his pocket. He has a weedy voice, husky yet high pitched, Home Counties turned Mick Jagger, "It's great stuff, just came in, I've done some cooking, they've tried it." Paddy has eyeliner on, glossy vinyl trousers that match his shirt, and a purple satin sash, that could be a decorative sling for a broken arm, or second rate beauty contest runner-up prize. Elsbeth reaches symbiotic, so as removed it must be replaced with systems for sustainability. In a way I'm relying on your DNA, and willpower, for your head to re-construct itself, and that part will take several months, perhaps even a year. For a significant time your whole brain, everything, will be on the outside, you have to be kept in a completely sealed environment, I am bringing in my own specialist nurses, two, the girls here wouldn't cope. You have the choice to carry on the way you are, it will get worse, you'll lose your sight, so on, and sooner or later your disorder will kill you, you probably won't reach thirty, I have seen this before. Either that, or we make very radical outcomes. It is space-age development Mr. Biancho." ConeBoy is tiring, he doesn't realise what's just been said. "What about my cone?" Menglees faces ConeBoy again, "Ah, that's the challenge, it's really clever what they did, you know, your team, in the eighties. I am having the same built by the dentist here, it's what they use in dental implants, where the bone has withered, they graft bovine matter, cadaver, then we'll re-connect you up, the breathing will be totally natural, no more valves, and a nose will grow around it." ConeBoy is nearly done with the pep-talk, he can't wait, "And what will I look like?" Menglees takes a long look at the twenty-four year old, taps his pencil on the desk, a rock 'n' roll beat, "Kid…

anything you want, they got it right here in the USA."

CHAPTER 23 - ANY SECOND NOW

"Ceneri alle ceneri, polvere alla polvere." ConeBoy plunges into the deep hole, it's slippery, mud falling in, and lunges at the coffin, the rain pours, unable to get a word out, yet screaming, he clasps the side of the box, hugging it, face pressed, his back is heaving, he's as close as he can get. The surface is shiny, varnished, buffed to an inch. The priest, black like Lucifer, black biretta, is soaked, continues, undeterred. Gash and Johnno go in after ConeBoy, drag him out, three plastered in the red clinging mire. They support him between them, Kate to their left, the only one with an umbrella, pulls it over to try and keep the water off, they huddle. ConeBoy looks to the sky, then at the stone;

DJANGO ALESSANDRO BIANCHO

1943 - 2006

RIPOSARE IN PACE

ConeBoy looks to heaven, rain drips from his Homeric chiselled nostrils, and bellows, clear, loud, his voice is male, a slight Tuscan lilt, ringing, ascending "DADDY!! DADDY!!" The holy-man bends, takes a clod, throws it into the hole, it thuds on the lid, and it's Gash's cue. He leaves ConeBoy, Max replacing him, and goes to the boombox, sat on a small foldable table, covered with clear polythene keeping the wet out, and presses play. The Who's 5:15 clinks in, the Waterloo train doors thud, and Towsend's Gibson SG picks out its transcendence. Gash breaks, disabled by grief, his legs give way, Ali steadying him.

A mob are being held back by the Carabinieri, the police have formed a line of motorbikes and cars dividing the crowds and the tiny graveyard site, lines of cameras at the front, soaked, newsmen, and photographers awaiting their stab. The tightly packed marble slabbed tombs repel the deluge, it's just another inclement on the Montaione hillside cemetery. Waterproofing is in short supply, the skies opened, turning the burial into a mud-bath skate-rink. There's an un-written embargo, and the Carabinieri are glowering at the assembled masses ensuring it's being adhered to. Long range lenses are idle on tripods, television cameras not rolling, anchors stand in suits sticking to prickly skin. Kate and Max are the main clothes-rail with ConeBoy's outfit hanging zipped in a travel garment bag, a vase of flowers, fruit-bowl, and fridge, only containing water and sodas. Vorderman is standing, beaming, tight jeans, heels, and a white top with v-cut flaps that extend over her jeans and corresponding lapels. It is cut low. "It's bloody good," she raises the hard-back, the jacket is Django's sharpie pen portrait, courier new bold print announcing the title;

CONEBOY

"Thank you Carol," ConeBoy is meek, bordering taciturn, the cocaine doesn't have that much effect, because of the powerful prescriptions he's on, "that's because of these guys, it was a mess Carol, before Faber got involved, I can't write," ConeBoy indicates to the girl, who's just out of University. Carol is embarrassed, she'd absolutely by-passed ConeBoy's literary appendage. "Susan Milne, from Faber," a high reedy Yorkshire voice, the small tubby bespectacled nerdy looking girl in vintage wear, greasy bobbed mop, polkadot skirt and manly 1950's shirt, stands, and they shake vigorously. ConeBoy is lolling on the relaxing settee, with water bottle, plain white t-shirt, crumpled SuperDry jeans, and Timberlands. Susan has taken the tubular framed ergonomic leatherette seat by the desk and mirror, and she reverses, resuming her post. ConeBoy continues, "So you liked it? You read it?" Carol responds, using it as an excuse to sit on the sofa, budging up close, "Oh, yes, I tend to dip, I get so much to read, you understand?" she looks for confirmation from Susan, and gets it in an enthusiastic nod, "they're making a film?" ConeBoy is reticent, adding to his allure, "Well, my agent's talking to people, there's -", Carol is effervescent, touching his leg, "And who's going to play you?!" ConeBoy grabs her hand on his leg, "Maybe me!" Vorderman falls about, belly laughing, intentionally rocking in to ConeBoy. She'd have sex with him there and then if literary-girl wasn't with them. Vorderman gets right back in, before any awkwardness can intercede, continuing the hand-clasp, "*Carol's Conundrums* is lightweight, a bit of fun in the afternoons, topical issues affecting our age demographic, and a few puzzles thrown in to keep them on their toes!" ConeBoy shakes his head, a hint of a pure perfect smile, and she does her business, "They'll be questions about the book, your life, nothing too heavy. It's aimed at a daytime audience, so there's areas we don't go, you happy with that? Halfway through Jade Goody will come in, then a break, and Coleen Nolan in the last section, and we'll do the quiz, you won't even know you're on television!" Carol looks about, like there are other people in the room, "Right! Make-up! You're all done I see," she pats his leg with the spare hand, further up, on his thigh, "and we'll see each other after, for a drink?" She goes in for the triple media kisses, ConeBoy reciprocates, not quite touching her cheeks, "Yes, love to Carol, look forward to it." She exits and ConeBoy flips his head up, slightly disdainfully, jet hair flows, "Jesus, nothing's changed." Susan inspects her smart-phone, "You're up to half a million followers on Twitter, let's see what this show does, she's really popular you know."

ConeBoy is in a fresh blue vertically striped shirt, fitted, it's a silk mix, with high collars, and wardrobe gave it the once-over with an iron just before he stepped out. His trousers are black, but tapered, narrowing to Chelsea boots that are on the chunky masculine sonar. He's relaxed, funny, teli is a cinch. He is upright, so the shirt complements his flat tummy, but his legs are crossed over, near Carol. She's changed into yellow suede crumpled boots with a hefty heel that sit below her knee, and a green Roland Mouret dress, short enough for her side of fifty. There is chemistry, and the afternoon bunch can sense it, the crowd is uproarious, book sales are off the scale, and Susan stands side-set in frumpy brown brogues, watching the floor monitor, and her blood pressure, at the rising Twitterdom quotas. The set is cheap, but looks fabulous on screen, kaleidoscopic bookcases, hordes of chintzy knick-knacks, a 1950's Gaggia, two bikes up on Seinfeld wall hangers, mocked-up distressed brickwork, and fake reclaimed chrome and ribbed glass factory-floor lights suspended above their heads. It's how everyone lives; in fabulously tasteful New York Greenwich Village converted warehouse apartments. "JADE GOODY!" Carol and ConeBoy rise at Carol's introduction, face the oncoming guest, she's high heeled, up on the catwalk, a massive grin, waving both hands at the welcoming cheer. A short pink dress with black ribbing combos sheeny bow shoes. It has her JG logo. The lone camera follows her across the floor, a single camera presentation, ConeBoy and Carol know they're off camera, and she slips him her phone-number, in to his pocket. Jade is up, but not before slavering over ConeBoy, and making a meal of him in front of the audience, "Ain't he HOT!"

The cattle moo in concert. "Fashion range darling!" is Carol's opening gambit, tearing Jade away, and Jade needs no encouragement to spill the beans on her new venture. Carol and ConeBoy let her rip it up, he's gentlemanly as well, and he only injects quips when Carol ties him back in to the action. "We'll be right back, with COLEEN NOLAN!" The monkeys go ape, and they hit the adverts. The runner shunts on with water, they slurp, the studio lights making a muck of their hydration. Carol offers her half-time orange halves, "Fantastic, you're both fantastic darling." Jade is energised, "We love him don't we!" Carol responding with a beady eye, "Hands off darling!" The floor manager starts the countdown, signals the crowd, and whooping drowns her, "Five, four, three, two, one", and Carol's on it, "COLEEN NOLAN!"

If the unwashed clapped and screamed anymore then the British Red Cross would be needed, as Coleen gets the amassed approval rating of ten thousand per-cent. Carol, Jade and ConeBoy do the upstanding, Coleen is heavy, quite obese, and crowbarred into an inadvisable tight black dress, with short black boots. There's continental luvvie greetings, and Coleen also bags ConeBoy, grabbing the book he's holding, raising it above her, nodding and pointing, attesting to its amazing'ness. ConeBoy's slight bashfulness is a hit, and she gives him a big banger of a kiss before taking the third seat which has been hastily thrust on set. She bangs on about her solo tour, flicking her long black hair, and blowing the fringe out of her eyes, that has been placed there to divert from her frowny forehead. Carol, the exemplar of slickness makes the concluding rounds of all three before the final-fun mini-quiz, which involves the guests and much jocularity, since no-one knows anything about mathematics, except Vorderman. "My thanks to ConeBoy - he's back!" ConeBoy raises his book, waving. The mummies in the tiered seating go ape-crazy. Jade's caught in the moment, and in her sweet and un-affected way, turns, and gives ConeBoy a lovely kiss, her hands affectionately holding his cheeks. She pulls away and a large cleft of his face pulls off. She looks at the slab of flesh in her hand, which includes a good part of his nose, and screeches a thin terrified moan.

THE END

Printed in Poland
by Amazon Fulfillment
Poland Sp. z o.o., Wrocław

55102491R00214